I0629648

MUKBANG

Alyanna Poe

Halloween 2023

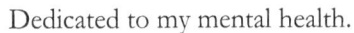

Dedicated to my mental health.

Contents

Introduction by Mike Salt

When I first met Alyanna I didn't know what to expect. She was insanely motivated about her unreleased book, which ended up being Eaten. I remember reading it and being blown away, not only by the fact that someone so young could write something so impressive, but the fact that it wasn't just good for someone that was so young… it was just good period. She had plenty to say from the moment I met her.

In the years that followed, I've watched her expand her presence. She didn't just write a followup, but she continued to grow and change as an author. She continues to try new things out, even if it doesn't always work. She isn't afraid of a challenge.

When she told me she was going to write Muk, I had no idea what I was in for. Of course it's well written, but you can really see how much she's turned a page in her already impressive skill set.

She is an author I will always have my eyes on and will always be one of the first people lined up to buy whatever she produces.

Watch out for her.

Mike Salt - Author of the Linkville Horror Series

Chapter One: A Ramen Shower

Glaring lights illuminated a mass of writhing flesh. Only the sounds of wet, sloppy squelching and heavy grunting filled the air. The room stunk of ramen, chili sauce, and sweat.

Jack had chosen to take his shirt off for this live stream, and Mia looked on, aghast. A lake of noodles drenched in a spicy, red sauce lay out before him. He took his chopsticks and twirled a mound of noodles onto them. Opening his mouth wide, exposing yellowed teeth, Jack stuffed them in. He quickly swallowed, the trail of noodles slipping through his closed lips with a slurp. On his chin, they left behind a red trail that dripped onto his bare chest.

"*Mmm,* that's good," he said, smiling.

He repeated the process, this time closing his eyes and moaning a bit as he swallowed. The sea of noodles hadn't been dented. Jack had a long way to go.

And the camera was there to catch it all.

Mia clutched the pendant on her necklace as Jack grabbed his Big Chug. He sucked on the fat straw, holding the cup with both hands and staring directly into the camera. He slurped on the soda for a good minute before breaking for air, taking a deep breath and exhaling with a loud belch. Jack forced a blush, holding a hand over his mouth and saying, "'*scuse me*," in a high-pitched voice. He spun his chopsticks around and around in the noodles, the wet sound sending chills down Mia's spine.

Collecting a ball of noodles bigger than Jack's oversized mouth, he forced them between his lips, looking deep into the camera. He turned his head to the side, showing the profile of him packing the noodles in. He pulled the loaded chopsticks away then thrusted them back in repeatedly, rolling his eyes back.

Mia sighed, her eyes falling to the carpet at her feet.

Jack finally stuffed the noodles in, taking great effort to chew and not have the bulk of noodles come spilling out of his maw. He felt strangely aroused as he stared back at himself in the small screen of his phone. There was a nauseous pit forming in his stomach, yet his loins burned.

Hearts floated across his screen as viewers liked the video, and Jack's heart fluttered.

People like that, huh? Let's give them a little more.

Jack slowly dipped the tips of his fingers into the oily sauce and pulled them back. He ran them across his bare chest in small circles, smirking into the camera. Mia looked at her husband as he leaned his head back, rubbing sauce onto his neck. She shook her head, thinking of the bath she would have to give him later.

The lights bore down on Jack's skin, showing every pore and hair follicle, every wrinkle and fold. He was the star of this show, and boy was it something to be present for.

Set against a textured, orange wall that Mia had painstakingly painted to Jack's every demand, the bald man sat in his electric wheelchair, his body overflowing the armrests. His neon green cast hid under the table, fitted to his leg. Sauce dripped onto his lap as he dipped both his hands into the bowl and smeared it about himself. His eyes found the camera lens, and he imagined the thousands of people he was staring at as he licked his fingers slowly. Jack inserted his index and middle finger into his mouth. He rolled his tongue over and around them, intently gazing at the camera.

He hadn't been intimate with his wife in months, but something about what he was doing gave him more pleasure than he thought she was capable of giving him.

Mia's eyes were glued onto this man. This man was her husband. She agreed to love him, in sickness and in health. But—

What is this shit?

Comments flowed in the corner of his screen. Thousands of people were watching the live stream. Mia knew how large Jack's audience was, and wondered if people felt the same way she did as they watched. She was full of disgust and anger, but most of all, she was curious why Jack felt the need to do this to himself. Imagining the hordes of people gawking at their screens—at her husband—made tears rise to the surface. She pushed them down, fearful of Jack's gaze.

Jack wiped his hands clean with a towel Mia had laid out for him. This wasn't the first time he made a mess of himself. He reached for his phone, a signal for Mia. She ran over to the table. Her shoes on the carpet made for silent travel. She released the phone, cradling it over the ocean of ramen and praying it didn't fall, just to set it into Jack's hands, making it appear that he grabbed it himself.

Had he been in better health, he could have bent further and reached across the table for it, but Mia knew that wasn't an option for him.

"*Hmm,* let's look at the comments, guys!" Jack squealed.

Mia's shoulders pulled up to her neck as she walked back to the hallway. She scrunched her nose and decided not to be present for the reading.

It's always the worst part.

"User *urmahmee.mycaulk* says, '*Wow, what a great live stream today!*' Thanks, *urmahmee.mycaulk!*" Jack dipped a finger into his ramen and sucked off the sauce as he read the next comment. "User *cashmeinside* said, '*That ramen looks spicy!*'" Jack laughed, the camera close to his face now. Viewers could view up his nostrils. The rolls of his neck jiggled as he laughed. "They're not *too* spicy!"

Suddenly the smile was ripped from his face. His eyebrows first lifted, then came crashing down over hardened eyes. His pulse hastened, throbbing in his chest.

Jack took a deep breath and spat, "*Well, User over18, let's see you get half a million subscribers on your channel.*"

The heat of the room finally took precedence in his mind. The sauce mixed with his sweat, leaving a greasy, red shine on his body. Every roll and crease felt slippery, and Jack felt as if he were about to pop out of his wheelchair like pus out of a pimple.

He looked over at the exceedingly full bowl of ramen. He hadn't even touched the three dozen halves of hard-boiled eggs yet, and those were an audience favorite.

Jack sighed, the weight of his body bearing down on his lungs. Holding his phone in one hand at arm's length, he picked up his chopsticks with a smile. The live stream had ten thousand viewers.

I can't quit now.

He slurped on noodles, watching more comments flood in. Some were endearing and cheerful, others hateful, and some bordered on sexual perversion. Viewers from all over the world watched, some in awe, some in terror, and some even watching with a hand between their legs.

Mia stood in the kitchen. Their house was of good size for a couple: small enough to be affordable for two people; big enough to allow them their own separate space. The internet had paid for this house. Not what Jack was currently doing, but the things they used to do as a couple. They agreed on a moderately priced home and renovated with sleek white marble, faux obviously, and stainless-steel appliances. The floor was charred oak, put in to replace the old, nasty carpet this place once had.

This floor had taken many scratches from Jack's new wheelchair and many dings from all the things he liked to throw. Out of the whole house, Mia related most to the floor.

Two big pots sat diagonally from each other on the stove, the water inside them dingy and foamy. A few noodles clung to the bottom helplessly.

Mia tapped each pot tentatively, checking if they were still hot. Discovering they were of grabbable temperature, she took each to the large, stainless-steel sink—the one that made her feel like she was working there rather than living there—and poured them down the drain. She looked out at the living room as she dumped them. Her blanket and pillow were in disarray on the couch. A night of restlessness was spent before waking up to Jack's screams.

"*Mia! Mee-uuuuh!*"

She had heard the shrieks in her dreams before coming to full consciousness. Dashing off the couch, she could only imagine the situation.

Did he finally roll off that bed and hurt himself? I told him not to buy that bed frame when we looked at it. Maybe his CPAP fell off, and he can't breathe. Dear God, please, no…

Their bedroom door was open, and there Jack lay in bed. An array of hoists and pulleys dangled from the ceiling, like a baby's mobile. He was breathing heavily, and Mia quickly grabbed his hand.

"What's wrong?"

Jack narrowed his eyes, scrutinizing her without a word. Dread piled up in Mia's stomach. Her words hung in silence until he spoke: "Have you started the ramen?" His tone was even, level, and calm, but she knew he knew the answer, and when he heard the answer, he would snap.

So, she lied.

"Yeah, the water is boiling *right now.*" She gave a sheepish smile, waiting again.

"Mmm, good." He smiled. The man she married was deep in there, under all the fat and sweat and anger. She could see him in Jack's smiles, so little were they directed at her anymore.

Jack had leaned back and dozed off right in front of her. His CPAP mask was crooked, but fearing waking him, she ran downstairs and started to boil water.

Packets of ramen and sauces were scattered around the counter, dusting the white acrylic in red powder. She picked each of them up, balling them into her hand and counting.

I made him fifteen packages of ramen this morning.

Mia could taste the salt on her tongue; she could feel his heart clenching in his chest.

He's going to die.

Wiping the counter free of splatters and picking up dishes, Mia wondered how long Jack was going to live. Tears sprouted in her eyes.

I'm going to kill him.

She shook her head, thinking of the pantry. She walked over to the tall door, apprehensive. Opening the door revealed three entire shelves filled with packages of ramen. Mia snatched a packet off the shelf and read the nutrition label.

1,800 milligrams?

Pulling out her phone, she searched: *healthy sodium intake per day.*

That's almost the daily intake.

And I just fed him twenty-seven-thousand milligrams of sodium.

Jack held the phone at an arm's length still. He could feel his arm burning, the skin jiggling as he fought to hold on. Noodles entered his mouth like an endless river, pooling in his gut like mating snakes. Although he couldn't taste the sauce anymore—his taste buds had died three months earlier after a multitude of habanero challenges—Jack could feel the inferno building in his abdomen. He thought he could hear his asshole crying, certain of its perilous future. A future full of burning and regret.

The number of viewers had gone down steadily as the stream continued. He thought about pulling a stunt to get more people interested, but deep in his straining heart he knew he had hit his peak for the day. He ate slowly but deliberately, gnawing away at the sea of noodles and hard-boiled eggs laid out before him.

The heat of the chili peppers was bearing down on him. His body glistened with sweat, the red sauce having been washed off in waves of bodily fluids long ago. The diaper he wore was drenched and expanding, yet not a drip of piss had left his urethra.

Halfway through the bowl of ramen, Jack wondered why he did it. He wondered why he gave up his previous life to make videos on the internet, but more hearts flooded in, and a comment caught his eye.

Talking around a mass of noodles, Jack read it aloud, "User *iheartjack* said, *'You're an inspiration to foodies everywhere. I hope to one day meet you.'*" He smiled, noodles squirming around in his teeth like fearful worms attempting to escape a bird's beak. He pitched his voice higher and said, "Aw, thank you, *iheartjack*."

He made note that *iheartjack*'s profile picture was him.

A warm feeling emanated from his chest, something other than heartburn, although there was a lot of heartburn. Not all the Tums in the world could help him now. Yet he smiled. If he could just get more followers like them. Followers that cared about him. Followers that saw him as more than just a man who ate on camera.

If I can just gain enough followers, maybe I'll feel like a man again, he thought, stuffing half a hard-boiled egg into his mouth.

By this time in the live stream, Jack was red-faced from effort, drenched in sweat, and tired. He had about a third of the bowl left.

I can do it. I have to do it.

People were leaving the live stream by the tens and then by the hundreds. Even those coming in couldn't balance out those leaving. Jack's heart sank. Laughing, he threw the chopsticks across the room, splattering the white wall in red sauce. It wasn't his mess to clean up anyway. He cupped his hand and dunked it into the bowl, gripping a handful of writhing noodles. Pulling them up like one would pull a clump of hair from the drain, he tilted his head and parted his lips like a baby bird. He fed himself the noodles. Red sauce rained down on his face, his mouth appearing to have had the worst menstrual cycle of its life. Jack audibly slurped them so unnecessarily, and he thought he saw the number stop.

Excitement grew, and he decided to complete the bowl, but not in an easy way to clean up.

"Be sure to share with your friends," he said, slurring his words and crossing his eyes, an attempt to seem silly that made most of his viewers cringe. Taking a handful of noodles, Jack draped them on his head like a bleeding wig. The sauce ran down into his eyes, burning all the way into his tear ducts. He screamed, making Mia jump.

She ran up the stairs, her slender figure easily bounding up two stairs at a time. Throwing herself through the doorway, she saw her husband: noodles sticking to his bald head, red sauce coating his face, ramen splattered on the floor and walls, looking like a bloody massacre. She froze. Jack flailed in frustration, his phone face down on the floor. Mia wasn't allowed in the room whilst Jack recorded, unless he called her over to move his phone around.

What do I do?

"MIA!" Jack shouted. His voice thundered through the room and through her chest. Viewers on the other end of his screen wondered what all the screaming was for, having only heard, *"Meee-aaaah!"*

She ran to his side, wiping frantically at his face with a nearby towel. His hands batted her away as he screamed. *"My phone! My phone!"*

Mia kept wiping his eyes, trying to get him to stop screaming.

"My phone!"

Seeing his Big Chug, Mia took the chance. She picked it up, drew her arm back, and sloshed it into Jack's face. His warbled screams shifted to a high-pitched squealing as she smeared the soda and sauce.

What am I doing with my life? she asked herself.

After crying the sauce out of his eyes, Jack looked at Mia with bloodshot eyes and demanded his phone. Only a foot from him, Jack could not bend down to retrieve it. She had given it to him. Jack checked the views and ended the stream with only fifteen viewers left.

Mia took a red-stained washcloth and wrung it out over the bath—the new bath Jack had hired some men to install recently. It was like those bathtubs with a door on them, the kind you see old people *walking* into on TV but double the width. With the help of Mia and *many* sturdy handles, Jack could pull himself from his wheelchair to the seat in the tub, where Mia washed him every night. She'd carefully bagged his leg's cast, hoping no more moisture could penetrate it and add to the smell.

Mia dragged the cloth across his neck roll, catching a new skin tag with the cloth and watching it bounce back.

That's new.

Crossing her mind was the image of taking her thumbnail and ripping the thing free. Instead, she took the cloth and scrubbed behind his ears.

Jack stared forward at the wall. He had a TV mounted there for his prolonged soaks, but tonight he needed silence. He listened to the water running and felt the warmth envelop him. His body was sore and tired, and he swore every time he breathed, one of his left ribs stung.

The smell of lavender Epsom salts brought back memories for Mia. She thought of their own *prolonged soaks* in the jacuzzi out in the backyard. The one that didn't even hold water anymore. She missed the days when he fit perfectly between her legs—the days when he wanted to be there. Moving in front of Jack's face and leaning down to show off the low scoop of her t-shirt, Mia kissed Jack on the cheek. He had been scrubbed free of ramen and chili and sweat, but he still smelled like it all, as if it were embedded within his pores, within *him*. It nauseated her, but Jack was her *husband*.

The least I can do is try.

"Can you hand me my phone?" Jack asked, refusing to make eye contact with her. His gaze remained fixed on the black television screen in front of him.

Mia turned around, sighing as she grabbed his phone from the bathroom counter.

"Don't drop it in," she said with a small giggle.

"*Don't treat me like a child*," Jack responded, a rubber ducky floating near his right, voluptuous breast.

Mia peered in through the pinkish water. A few noodles floated here and there, but she was looking deeper. A wave of flesh encapsulated Jack's body, hiding what used to be there.

"When was the last time we cleaned under your flap?" Mia asked.

Jack's eyebrows furrowed, and he slowly looked up from his phone, glaring. "*What?*"

Mia realized her folly. "Oh, well, it's just been a while since we really *got in there*, ya know?"

Jack looked at her smugly. "Just say you're horny, *Mia.*" He grabbed at one of the washcloths floating around the bath and pulled it to his chest. "*I'm tired and ready for bed.*" His eyes didn't leave his phone screen as Mia finished bathing him.

She drained the bath, knowing damn well that even though the water was a rancid color, Jack was not entirely clean. Invisible bugs crawled on her skin as she thought about the lint and many forms of bacteria that lay between his rolls.

Dear God, his penis must smell like a cheese cave.

A voice in the back of her mind whispered, *and how I'd let it slip inside me.*

Mia stiffened, that nauseous pit in her stomach swirling and rolling like a catfish in muddy water. The water was drained, and Jack was asking for help out of the bath as he attempted to stand, but Mia was frozen in place. The hot smell of his body filled her lungs. She looked over at him, seeing him not as her husband, but as a steaming dumpling full of rotten meat and twisting worms.

The white tile below her opened up, revealing a fresh grave. Chili sauce poured out of the bath and into the grave. Jack— now a doughy dumpling with arms and legs—stood up on his feet, something he hadn't done alone in months, and twirled like a dancer. He hopped up onto the edge of the bathtub and swan-dived into the pool of sauce in the grave, not splashing a drop out of it.

Then she was back in the bathroom, staring at her husband as he yelled at her. She quickly wrapped a towel around his waist and helped him into his chair. Heat radiated off his body, steam making it hard to breathe. Jack sat in his chair, gasping, while Mia's mind explored a time long ago.

"Mama?" Mia could hear Jack snoring in bed, his CPAP machine hissing. She moved down the hallway in her socks, gently stepping around the boards that she knew creaked.

"Mia, it's late. Are you okay?" Mia's mother, Roxanne, said, her voice groggy.

Mia hesitated, her throat tightening and tears welling in her eyes. Could she really tell it all? Every intimate detail? And would it even help her?

"Mama, I think Jack is dying."

Roxanne gasped, getting out of bed and pulling on a coat while Mia's father slept. "Why do you say that?"

It had been three years since Mia had seen her parents. A lot had happened in three years, including a viral video that had changed Jack's mindset. Mia learned to put her feelings aside for Jack, something her mother had done for her father.

"He's just eating so much, and he's gained so much weight." She paused, trying to get her mouth to catch up with her thoughts. "He refuses to see the doctor."

Roxanne stood outside on her porch in North Carolina, an entire country away from her daughter. The porch was old and weathered, similar to how she felt. She laughed, shaking her head. "Oh, he's not dying. Just put him on a diet." She laughed a bit louder. "Or even slip some weight loss pills into his dinner."

The thought of it made Mia sick. In a serious tone, she said, "Mom, I think his heart would explode."

Roxanne scoffed. "Oh, come on, how much weight has he gained?"

I guess she doesn't keep up with Jack's channel.

"I'll—I'll send you a photo." Mia pulled her phone away from her ear, not daring to put her mother on speaker. She opened her mother's messages and scrolled through her photos. A kind reporter had emailed Jack, but that was something that Mia dealt with. He asked some questions, just a short, written interview about Jack's channel and what he did, along with requesting some photos. Mia decided to take these photos with her phone and email them, too.

While taking said photos, Mia thought about some advice her mother had told her as a teenager:

Some days you need to see your life from the outside. Step into another's shoes and see how they would see your life. How do you feel about the person you see?

Her thumb hovered over a photo of Jack. There he sat in front of packages of marshmallows. It had been Marshmallow Monday, a segment he did every first Monday of the month. He was very specific about his schedule.

She was torn between two photos. The one of Jack sitting in front of the marshmallows with a grin on his face—again, she saw the old Jack sitting underneath all those layers of skin and meat—and one of him stuffing marshmallows into his face, his mouth like a black hole for junk food. They both showed his recent weight gain, but one—one showed something else.

Mia chose the photo of him stuffing his face. She waited a few seconds, listening to her mother fumble with her phone.

"*Oh!*" Roxanne shook her head. "Oh, no, baby, that's not Jack...*is it?*"

"It is."

"*What happened?*"

"Later—tomorrow—look up *Jack Eats the Box.*" Mia's face burned. She was ashamed, sad, and unsure what to do.

"*Jack Eats the Box?*" Roxanne asked.

"Yes."

Mia's eyes stung, the whites of them bloodshot. The clock on the side table beside the couch where she slept read *one 'o eight* in neon green digital numbers. A video played out on her screen, as hundreds had in the hours she sat in the dark.

"Hi, I'm Jack and this is Mia. We're the Travelers, and today we're in Tokyo taking you on a tour of the finest shops. Will we buy any merchandise?"

Jack hesitated, letting Mia tune in.

"We just might as our first sponsor has generously donated a thousand dollars for us to use here in the biggest metropolis in the world!"

Mia sniveled. A young, newlywed couple, and so cute. That's what they used to be. Jack was cut and clean, his body tone and his hair always so neat. The video was grainy, but their smiles shone through it all. They had lost all of it in the span of three years.

Maybe it all started to end before Covid.

Mia looked at herself. The video had cut to her trying a dress on that, at the time, she knew was too expensive for her. She had been nervous trying on clothes she knew she couldn't afford. The proprietor of the business had watched over them like a hawk, sure that he tended to their every need, and she didn't even have half the dress's cost in her pocket.

Do it for the fans, she remembered thinking.

Is that what Jack thinks every time he forces himself to eat a meal meant for ten people?

The heater kicked on, startling her. Their house lay set back in the cool pines, generally covered in mist. Moving from North Carolina to Northern California had been rough at first, but this house was so beautiful.

Was it worth it though?

Worth what?

Your husband dying.

Mia thought back to meeting Jack. They weren't high school sweethearts, and they hadn't had a meet-cute in a cafe. No, they had met online back in the days of reckless nudes and thick black eyeliner. Jack's shirtless photos had caught her eye, and he'd been in the market for an emo girl.

You miss those days, don't you?

Who wouldn't?

The days of getting to know each other, progressing into traveling the world together and being funded by strangers on the internet. It was a *dream*.

The video played on, this time showing Jack speaking in Japanese to an older man. At the time, Mia thought he looked ancient. Looking back at it ten years later, she saw he was most likely only in his sixties. They had dubbed over a horrible translation, and the conversation went as:

Jack: "So, where do you see yourself in ten years?"

The old man, later introduced as Makoto: "Ten years?"

Jack: "Yeah, what do you think your future holds?"

Makoto: "I don't think about those things." He shook his head, looking at the ground.

Mia had chimed in: "Well, Jack and I like to think we'll be big internet celebrities in ten years, maybe even—"

Mia slammed the laptop shut. She didn't even check to see if she'd cracked the screen because who cares?

She sat in stunned silence, a single thought racing through her mind.

How have I let this happen?

Chapter Two: Vanilla Morning Sex

"*Ice cream?* This early in the morning?" Mia had prepared an oiled pan to make her usual fried eggs—two for her, ten for Jack.

"*You heard me!* Now hurry up, I want to start *recording!*" Jack said through the screen on her tablet. Then the screen flipped to her wallpaper as Jack hung up. She wondered how he could sound so demanding and whiny at the same time.

Digging around the freezer, she realized how many choices there were. She didn't remember buying this much ice cream.

Didn't even tell me what flavor he wants.

Mia chose vanilla and grabbed a large metal spoon. As she carried the quart upstairs, she questioned herself.

Why am I doing this? When am I going to talk to him? Is this really what he wants?

There Jack sat.

He's sitting up by himself?

"Here's your ice cream. Turns out we had a lot—"

"Thank you. Can you close the door on your way out?" Jack yanked the ice cream from Mia's hands and stuck the spoon in his mouth. His phone was propped up on a pillow.

Mia left the room without a word, wondering how he managed to set all that up by himself.

He even removed his mask himself.

In the past few months, Jack had been incapable of doing anything. Mia felt as if she were caring for a three-hundred-pound toddler rather than living with her husband. Walking down the stairs, she could hear him start his morning intro.

"Gooood morning, fans, followers, subscribers, and worshipers." He paused for a smile. "This morning, rather than eating those bland fried eggs, I'm having ice cream in bed!"

Jack grew silent as people were trickling into the live feed, *and the feasting began.*

Ripping off the lid, he tossed it aside with a grunt, splattering ice cream onto Mia's side of the bed. He licked his lips slowly. Holding the quart from the bottom with one hand and his spoon with the other, he leaned down and licked the surface of the ice cream, swirling his tongue around as he kept eye contact with the camera. Soft, wet noises managed to make their way through viewers' speakers.

As more users entered the stream, more commented, wishing him a good morning or a good day.

In a low voice, one that was at one point only reserved for Mia in the bedroom, he said, "Good morning, everyone."

He scooped at the ice cream, a voice in the back of his head telling him to yell at Mia later for grabbing him vanilla. Jack heaved a large chunk of it out—a bite that would surely be too large for his mouth—and dove at it. He bit it, sinking his teeth into the hoard. Rearing his head back like a wolf tearing into a carcass, he chewed with his mouth open, cream dripping from his lips and chin.

And there she was, his regular: user *iheartjack.*

"*Good morning, Mr. Jack. I wonder how that ice cream tastes,*" followed by a heart-eyed emoji.

Jack felt a beast inside of him. People like user *iheartjack* empowered him. She had been a long-time follower of his. Many times, she commented how she had seen all his travel vlogs with his wife and all his current videos. He told his followers to never speak of those vlogs.

He took another bite out of the ice cream, pulling away with a slurp.

White noise and sloppy sounds were all viewers had to look forward to, yet thousands were eagerly watching.

Jack's ribs throbbed. His recent fall down the stairs flashed through his mind. Brief embarrassment heated his face. More than his leg had been broken down the unforgiving staircase. His ribs ached with each of his labored breaths, and as he ate quickly and breathed between bites, his entire side throbbed.

The strain of forcing down gulps of the frozen treat and the heater on full blast began to melt him. A blend of soupy ice cream and sweat mingled on his skin. He grunted like a wild animal as he stuffed more into his mouth.

Out of the corner of his eye, he could see the viewers and likes and comments pouring in, so he took his hand, much like a child would, and ripped out a fistful of ice cream. He eyed the camera and ate from his palm, a mess dripping onto his lap. Slurping and moaning, he closed his eyes, fully embracing the ice cream in his hand like a lover. His tongue danced across the surface, blindly searching for something. It curled around lumps of ice cream and his fingers, pleasuring his taste buds with the flavors of vanilla and salt.

From somewhere in the southern part of California—a day's drive from Jack's home—a young woman watched in the darkness of her room. Curtains kept out the morning sunshine as she propped up her phone against a book on her desk.

Jack's grunts prickled her ears. She couldn't take her eyes off him. Her plump chest heaved in excitement, the anticipation burning in her thighs. She twirled a finger in her dark, curly hair as she thought.

Should I do it?

Could I do it?

His DMs are open…

Through the small screen, she could see Jack look at the camera—look at *her*. Her heart fluttered. Jack closed his eyes and gently kissed the mound of ice cream.

I never thought I'd want to be ice cream so bad.

Getting up, she sauntered to her nightstand. A drawer was calling to her. She opened it with numb fingers, her heart pounding.

I'll do it after.

She nodded.

I'll do it after.

Her hand slipped into the void, and out she pulled a rabbit. Neither fuzzy nor warm, she would welcome its embrace, nonetheless. Sitting on her bed on her knees, she turned the rabbit on and watched the screen.

Jack desperately awaited the bottom of the carton. His fingers had scraped and clawed at the ice cream, numbing them. He felt the approach of vanilla flavored slosh approach his esophagus. Forcing it down with another handful of ice cream, Jack wondered what he was doing.

In front of his reflection, a comment appeared.

"*Love seeing you living your best life!*" from user *iheartjack*.

She was a beautiful girl. Long, dark hair. Light brown skin. The deepest brown eyes—almost black. Just the look of her lips made his mouth water. Jack visited her page often. He always thought that if he could drive, he would go anywhere to see her—*to feel her.* He dreamed of her whispering sweet nothings into his ear in Spanish as he felt her soft skin.

Jack took another huge bite.

For her.

His fingernails finally scratched at the bottom. He had hoped he would finish the carton and leave the live stream triumphant.

The incessant white noise from the ceiling fan and wet chewing made viewers cringe. He smacked his lips with fervor, hoping to tantalize those viewers' senses. His views began to drop.

Like bodies off a skyscraper, people were leaving his stream. He had done as they asked. Ice cream for breakfast was the most sought-after video after sausage and milk, and he wasn't ready for sausage and milk. Jack panicked, struggling to get the last bit of ice cream out of the carton. He shoveled it into his open mouth, his fingers painfully grazing his teeth. After swallowing, Jack took a moment to catch his breath.

"*Fat ass!*"

It flashed across his screen so quickly that he almost didn't see it. Usually comments like that were deleted by the platform, but on live streams, it's something hard to control.

The number of viewers plummeted as he signed off.

"*I hope everyone had a good time! See you all later!*"

Why he had chosen to speak like a baby in all his videos, he didn't know, but it was his brand. People expected it. There were t-shirts with his face or bust on them with binkies and phrases people associated with him. "*I'm sowwy,*" being one of the best sellers.

The black screen stared back at him, sneering.

Losing your audience, Jacky? Can't keep them around to watch you gorge yourself?

Jack shook his head, one of his extra chins wobbling.

It's just a bad day for a stream. Everyone will be watching this evening's stream. They'll be there. They will.

He slid himself down in bed, staring at the ceiling fan. Rather than watching the blades spin round and round, he watched the center. His stomach warbled, calling to him from under a mound of flesh. He thought about the quart of ice cream in its liquid state, taking up all the real estate in his stretched-out gut. If he thought last night's spicy ramen shits were bad, he was in for a rude awakening. Long ago, Jack was convinced he was lactose intolerant, something that hadn't changed. His gut churned, and with each movement, it pushed sludge further up his throat.

Like a violent animal with no other means of escape, the ice cream came barreling up. He leaned over, moving faster than he had in a long time, and heaved it over the side of the bed. Pulling himself back into the bed and wiping his creamy lips, his head throbbed. Fatigue took over his body, weighing down his eyelids. He relaxed into his pillow and closed his eyes.

Mia heard the commotion, and there she stood on the other side of the door, listening. It was obvious she would have a mess to clean up, but she was terrified of walking in on him recording.

She was no longer in the picture in Jack's career. He had told her it was good for his followers to see him as a single man.

When Jack ripped his first snore, Mia knew she'd have to go in.

A splatter of melted ice cream and the remnants of last night's ramen besmirched the floor. Jack lay, a sleeping giant, in bed. His CPAP machine wasn't on. Mia scrambled, as quietly as possible, to get the mask on him. She wrestled with his large head, getting the straps around it and securing the mask in place.

Turning it on, she realized it had been a while since she'd cleaned it. As the air began to flow, Jack relaxed further into the bed in his comatose state. Mia shook her head, wondering how he slept through it all.

The white liner of the curtain billowed lightly as the fan spun in circles above her head. Grey light from the mist filtered sun washed the room. Mia looked at her husband.

Last time he was weighed, he rang up at 357 pounds. He had fallen asleep in only his towel, and most nights he refused the comforter or even a thin sheet. She couldn't remember where she had gotten a towel large enough to fit around his waist, but she could have sworn the listing showed a group of ten at the beach.

Every night for a year, she wondered if he would wake up.

Would it be better if he didn't?

Her eyes widened, tears welcoming themselves back home in her lids. She traced the outline of his body with those eyes, thinking how much he resembled a juicy maggot. Acne scattered his entire body, something she had tried to get rid of with vigorous scrubbing and harsh creams. Big boils of pus and scabs littered him, waiting to leak fluids on their sheets.

Do you think they taste sweet?

Her mouth puckered, and she shuddered.

He only eats fat and sweets. You'd think all his liquids would taste like butter.

Mia held back a gag, quickly stepping out of the room. Soon after, she came back with a bucket of water, rubber gloves, and a whole package of rags. She was thankful for the hardwood floor.

After soaking up what she could with dry rags and setting them aside, she wiped the floor down with a wet rag. Swirling her hand around over and over, she realized she was only chasing around the milky puddle. She dunked the rag back into the bucket and wrung it out, then dunked it back in. It splattered as it hit the boards, adding to the puddle. This was taking longer than she'd anticipated.

On her hands and knees, Mia frantically wiped at the floor, the water still discolored. Bits of noodles floated here and there, traveling far under the bed. A stagnant sea of bile and warm water, its turbulence only controlled by Mia's sporadic motions. The sea finally reached her knees, wetting her sweatpants. Tears dripped down into the milky ocean like rain.

What am I doing?

She stood up suddenly, dropping the rag into the puddle and splashing water about the room. No expression on her face, Mia left the room, tossing her rubber gloves back. Her sweatpants dripped water onto the floor as she dashed through the house. Droplets tickled her as they ran down her spindly legs.

At one point she had been a young model, then a travel vlogger, and then...

A caretaker for an unappreciative whale.

She floated downstairs, her face finally hardened into anger. At the couch, she ripped away her clothes, using her shirt to dry off. She pulled on the outfit she had set out for herself on the coffee table. Pulling her fingers through her chopped pixie cut, a remnant from her model days she refused to rid herself of, she snatched her car keys and purse.

The front door opened and closed silently as her breaths heaved in and out. The outside air embraced her in all its coolness, the gentle mist caressing her hot skin.

Pine trees.

She took a deep breath in, having not been outside in days.

No ramen. Or chili. Or sweat. Or musk. Or—

She hopped in her car, something Jack hadn't been able to do in over a year. The leather still emitted that new car smell, and she found herself at ease.

Mia would hit the gym first. She hadn't been there in almost a month, and her body yearned for it. Backing out of their asphalted driveway, she could feel a weight lifting off of her shoulders the further she inched away. Foot by foot, her tires carried her from her prestigious prison.

No more vomit. No more sweat. No more food. Just me. Me and my—

Her phone rang, startling her into slamming on the brakes. Her rear end was just hanging out onto the main road— something the county had created decades ago and barely took care of.

Jack's face, his old face, the one that didn't scream *I eat for strangers on the internet*, stared back at her, her ringer hollering into the cabin of her car.

Fuck him. Fuck it. I'm leaving.

She reached for her phone to shut it off, but something whispered in her mind.

In sickness and in health, Mia. Jack is clearly sick. What if he's hurt himself?

Mia looked up at the house, staring at the window Jack was surely behind, the mountain of meat that he was.

Tears streamed down her face. She just wanted to go to the gym, something that had been part of her regular schedule only months ago. Already she could feel the extra weight on her body. She could feel it in the way she moved, when she sat down, even in her eating habits. The mirror laughed at her every morning after she showered.

Did I even shower today?

The ringer was almost over when Mia made her decision. She slammed the car into drive and punched the gas, her tires squealing on the wet asphalt. The driveway was long, but surely not long enough to drag race on. She held the steering wheel tight, imagining herself flying through the front room's door, the impact blissfully killing her. The house approached fast.

At the last second available, Mia slammed the brakes. Her tires screamed again, bracing themselves for impact as they slid across the slick asphalt. She flew forward in her seat, having not put her seatbelt on yet, and her chest hit the steering wheel. The headlights grew larger in the front window as the car neared, and just a few inches from the glass, Mia's car stopped.

She sat stunned, gripping the steering wheel with white knuckles and panting.

Her phone lit up with Jack's face again.

If he's okay to call me again, he can wait until I get up there.

"Where were you?! Why didn't you answer your phone?!" Jack screamed as she walked into their bedroom.

Mia hadn't caught her breath before coming in, and the moist air restricted her lungs further. Without a word, she stepped to the windows on the other side of the room, threw back the curtain liners, yanked the blinds up, and opened the windows one at a time until all three were open.

Jack yelled at her, something about needing her to do this and that and prepare for tomorrow. Mia couldn't hear exactly what he was saying over the hum in her head.

How have I put up with this for three years?

Has it been going on since before his mukbang fad?

She stood, looking out the windows at the misty night. The sun glowed through the fog, like a train coming at her full speed. Jack's words bounced off her back. A particular night in Paris came back to her:

"You're wearing that?" Jack asked.

Mia looked at herself in the mirror. She wore a t-shirt and jeans. The t-shirt fit her well and the jeans weren't the cheap kind. She saw nothing wrong, and only wanted to match Jack, who wore cargo shorts, a t-shirt, and flip flops. Turning to him, she said, "Yeah?"

"Go change into a nice dress. We're in Paris for Christ's sake." He rolled his eyes and went out onto the balcony.

Comments like that came often. Having experience in the fashion industry and dealing with barking agents, Mia hadn't thought much of it.

I let it go too far.

Whipping around, Mia's eyes were alighted.

Jack's entire body bounced as he bellowed, the bed creaking beneath him.

Blood coursed through Mia's body and a sick smile crossed her lips.

"*I'm tired of smelling you,*" she said. It was quiet, but Jack stopped screaming.

"What?"

Mia approached the bed, feeling ten feet tall. "I. Am. Tired. Of. Smelling. *You.*"

A mix of horror, sorrow, and shame manipulated his face until he got it under control. "I don't *stink.*" His mouth had twitched to the side, yet his eyes remained stone cold.

She raised her arms, causing him to flinch. "*This house is nothing but a prison of filth and gluttony.* I'm ashamed to even live here." Her voice remained stable.

Jack's face twisted in anger. "You think this house is a prison for *you?*" he asked.

"Well, yeah. You always need me here, and I never have time to do anything for myself. I just—"

"*I can't even go downstairs in my own God damned house, Mia.*"

Mia's neck tensed. "*It's your own God damned fault for eating so much! You don't do anything but eat and eat and eat! It's no wonder gravity yanked you down the stairs like that! You're killing yourself, Jack!* And I can't help you anymore." She looked down at her hands, examining her wedding ring—the one that matched the one Jack no longer wore. "I quit."

Jack glared at her, his eyes two bottomless pits. "*What do you mean you quit?*"

She stood up, throwing her hands up. "*This, Jack!* I quit your videos. I quit cooking for you. I quit bathing you." The look on his face softened. "Jack, you can't expect me to watch—no, *help*—you kill yourself."

"Mia."

The tenderness in his voice caught her off guard.

"Besides my videos and following, I have *nothing.*"

A spear was thrown into her chest. "*Nothing?*" She threw her arms wide, gesturing at the house and herself at the same time. Jack shook his head. Mia felt herself losing control again. "*Then why'd you put a ring on my finger, Jack?!*" She bent down, sticking a finger in his face. Under her breath, she hissed, "*I didn't marry you to be your caretaker.*"

Standing back, she ripped the ring from her finger and slung it at him, hitting him square in the forehead. "*You're a WHALE, Jack! No one is going to love you the way I used to.*"

Jack's face contorted. He tore through emotions like a time lapse, from anger to crying to laughing. Mia watched in disgust, the hairs on the back of her neck standing up.

His face stilled, and he said, "If you think I'm going to choose you over a million followers across all my platforms...*you're stupid.*"

"I didn't think you would. Just be prepared to lose this house in court." She chuckled. "That is, *if you can get to court on your own.*" She laughed louder, cackling. "*You did this to yourself, Jack! Feed me more, Mia, feed me more for all my online weirdos!*" She clutched her stomach, the laughs jarring her insides. Stumbling over to him, she grabbed his fat cheeks and pinched them, laughing an inch from his face. He'd never seen her smile so wide before. "*What next, Jacky boy? You gonna construct a woman out of hot dogs and fuck her?!*"

Jack reached up to remove her hands from his cheeks when she shoved him back. His sweaty head smacked the headboard, and he cried out.

Mia's laughter couldn't be contained. "*Not that you could fuck anything! I'm sure your poor penis has lost all blood circulation.*" Her laughter turned to screams, and her knees buckled. She fell to her knees and slapped the floor with open palms. "*I can see it now!*" Pointing a finger at him, she yelled, "*You were afraid of me cleaning under your flap because you know your dick is sitting in there, detached! It's been sliding around in your fat rolls, getting more action than you'll ever get again!*" Rolling onto her back, she kicked her legs into the air, gasping.

Jack watched, wide-eyed, as she stopped laughing and caught her breath. She stood, instilling fear into Jack.

"Yes, Jackie, you've been running this circus *much* too long. It's mine now, and you're my thousand-pound *freakshow*." She caressed his cheek with a soft hand. "I don't quit anymore, honey. I take it *allll* back." Mia stooped down and kissed Jack on the cheek. "*Get some rest. We've got a lot of work to do this evening.*"

Chapter Three: Squirting Sausages

Sausages sizzled on the frying pans Mia put out. The house was heavy with the scent of frying meat. In the oven, a tray of meatballs, fresh from a frozen bag, cooked on high. Mia hummed, pulling two one-gallon jugs of milk from the fridge. She shimmied around, blasting music from a little Bluetooth speaker on the counter. Slipping her hand into a drawer, she retrieved a turkey baster.

Up and down the stairs she went, setting the stage for Jack's next video as he watched in horror.

"Surely we can do another video today, right?" he asked, reaching for her as she walked away.

Slipping out the door, she called back, "No! And don't call me *Shirley!*" She cackled on her way down the stairs.

His phone was set up, and rows and rows of sausages were pointed at him. Mia had chocked his wheelchair in place, trapping him.

Carrying the gallons of milk and clutching the turkey baster between her teeth, Mia ran up the stairs, beaming. She set everything down on Jack's banquet table, something just that morning she thought she would never do again.

It's kinda fun when you're in charge, she thought, practically dancing down the stairs.

Jack looked from his phone to the food in front of him, sweating. Mia had forced him into one of his crybaby shirts, and the places where it tucked into his creases were already wet.

I don't want to do this.

Jack wondered if he could walk. Just push himself away from this table and stand up like he could have a few months ago. He shook his head, knowing it was impossible with the cast on his leg which weighed down his mind more than his body.

"*Meatballs!*" Mia called from the staircase. Smiling ear to ear, she sashayed up, holding a pan of meatballs and wearing her favorite pair of oven mitts. She slammed the tray down in front of him, eyeing him the whole time.

He's scared.

He doesn't want to do it.

Her smile widened.

Perfect.

Using toothpicks, Mia arranged one sausage and two meatballs at a time until the table was full of makeshift, cooked cock and balls.

Jack looked on in horror. He shook his head. "That's not what the followers said they'd want to see."

Mia shrugged, filling up a big glass of milk and setting it beside the trays. "That's too bad." She paused, slipping a small pistol out from her waistband. "*Because I'd kill to see it.*"

The last time Jack had felt this terrified of Mia had been six years after they were married. After a bout of drinking in a small town in Ireland, Jack awoke to a knife at his throat. He had screamed, but someone covered his mouth. The side lamp in their hotel room clicked on, exposing a drunk and naked Mia crouching over him from her side of the bed. She had that same wild smile on her face, and she asked, "*You'd never cheat on me, would you Jackie?*" Her eyes had narrowed at the end of the question, and the pressure on his neck intensified, the blade digging a thin line through his skin.

He tried shaking his head, feeling the knife slice in further, then said, "*No.*"

Mia's smile retired to the gentle one it usually was—the kind, *I-love-you-dear* smile he had fallen in love with, and she said, "*Okay*," and tossed the knife aside.

Nothing had been said the next morning, or for the next five years.

Mia remembered the night well. She'd had nightmares about the night ending with her showered in the rain of her husband's blood, her drunken folly, the end of her marriage—the end of her life.

"Listen, Jack," she said, slipping the pistol back into her waistband, "we used to be partners in this show. We presented ourselves to the internet as—quite frankly—a power couple. Money. Fame. Traveling to the world's finest shops and sought-after restaurants." She sighed, sitting down in a chair almost across the room from him. Between the sweaty, salty fumes emanating from his body and the smell of plain, cooked meat, Mia was between throwing up her lunch and blowing the nose off her face with a bullet. "Now here we are. I cook for you and remain pent up in this house like your pet, and you get to gorge yourself on camera, connecting with people across the world. I miss that, Jack! I *miss* feeling connected to human beings other than you. We had the world in our hands."

Jack rolled his eyes. "*Mia.*" He paused, looking at the meat in front of him. "Mia, Covid stopped *all* travel."

She perked up. "*Yeah!* And I told you it was the perfect time to hit local places here in the US. Go on a road trip and find all the small businesses still open and fighting to serve this country. We could have helped so many small towns, Jack." Tears welled in her eyes.

Roxanne, and her father, Tim, practically raised Mia in their family Chinese restaurant, but when Covid hit, even Mia's donations couldn't save them. People had thrown bricks through the windows, blamed them for the start of something they were just as innocent to, and stopped supporting them or even smiling at them on the street. She was there when her parents handed the keys back to their landlord. She had to watch as her parents lost their livelihood.

Jack already knew what was going through her mind, but would she even consider his issues?

"My mom died of Covid, Mia. You really think I wanted to go out and chance either of us getting it just to eat at roadside shit-shacks?"

"*Oh, fuck you, Jack.*" She crossed her arms, her mind a swirl of emotions as, internally, she watched her mother crying as she took money from Mia to keep the lights on. "No, I suppose you'd rather we hole up in this house and I help you commit suicide by butter."

"*I didn't know I'd get this big!*" he screamed, a fiery pain spreading across his chest.

"Oh, yeah, eating for ten people three times a day, and you didn't know you'd get this big." She scoffed. "I swear you gain three pounds for every video you make. It's *disgusting* what you're doing to yourself—what you're doing to *me*." Mia stood up abruptly. "When was the last time you even fucked me? Or at the very least, made the move to do so?"

Jack's eyes widened. He licked his sweaty upper lip, thinking.

"*Exactly.*"

Jack huffed, his entire body jiggling. "Relationships aren't just about sex, you know. There's plenty of people out there who are asexual and still have partners and spouses."

Mia narrowed her eyes. "Oh, don't go there, you pompous *asshole*. What? Are you asexual now? Gone from fucking me nightly to abstaining due to sexual preferences?"

"I mean—"

"Tell me the *truth*, Jack." Her eyes bore into his even from across the room. "Why are we even married anymore?"

"I don't know! Okay? You said yes to all the videos and the cooking and the caretaking, so I thought you were okay with it."

Mia realized her lack of communication was partially to blame. It only came across physically as a flicker in her eyes, but she held fast, remaining stone cold.

No, he's manipulating you.

"*When was the last time you saw the doctor for your weight?*" she asked, her voice rising.

Jack threw up his hands. "*I don't know!*"

"*And how many times have I asked you to go?!*" Her voice came out as a hoarse scream, something neighbors would be sure to hear, if they had any.

Jack was catching on to the case she was making. "Well, how many times have I asked you to cook for me, and you've said yes?"

Mia thrusted her hands out in a shrug. "What am I supposed to do? Say no so you can scream at me?"

"*I do not scream at you!*" he roared.

"*You're doing it right now!*" she fired back, whipping the pistol from behind her back and aiming it at his forehead.

She imagined blowing the top right off his head, certain ice cream would splatter the wall. That's all he was made of: sugar and fat—like some fucked up kid's worst nightmare and sweetest dream combined, a zombie made of food. Chocolate sauce would ooze from his shattered scalp, running into his eyes and mouth. His tongue would circle his lips to get a taste before dying.

"*FUCK!*"

She squished her eyes closed, taking deep breaths. Opening them, she said, "We're doing the video, and we're doing it *now.*"

Jack faced the barrel of the gun, the pressure of a knife from his past stinging his neck. "Fine. I'll play into your power trip."

"Excellent," she said, walking over to his phone and putting her gun back into her pants. "Lights. Camera. *Action.*"

Jack started with his dinner opening, forcing a smile and trying not to sound like a gun was being put to his head. She *had* put the pistol away, but she could have his head in pieces within milliseconds if she wanted.

People began pouring into the stream. Little did Jack know, Mia had arranged a sausage in a glass of milk, with another sausage dripping milk beside it. She snapped a photo and posted it to all his platforms with the words *Sausage Party!* as the caption.

Jack's jaw almost dropped at the amount of people viewing within the first minute. He quickly introduced himself to any new followers and showed off his banquet with an arm opening gesture.

Mia watched directly behind the phone, her arms crossed. She stared down her nose at him.

I've finally confronted the beast.

Jack's stomach sank despite his elation at the number of viewers. Trembling, his hand reached for one of the sausage and meatball horror shows his wife expected him to eat. He realized with an entire body tremor that she had overcooked all of the meat, making the meatballs close to crumbling and the sausages deeply wrinkled. His only savior would be whole milk.

"*Bon appétit*," he said, the sausage nearing his lips.

Viewers watched in anticipation, others in disgust, and some in a deep state of arousal. Mia fought to keep a smile off her face, giddiness bubbling up from her gut.

First his tongue met the tip of the sausage, then he slid it into his mouth. Deep regret filled him. Staring into the camera, he took his first bite, that feeling of excitement he usually experienced while recording nowhere to be found. His mouth squelched as he chewed, like nails on a chalkboard to Mia. She made a motion to hurry up, and Jack chewed faster, swallowing the dry meat before he was ready. He took another bite, looking up to Mia as she seemed to fake being pleasured.

She's telling you to moan, idiot.

Everything within Jack said no, but he did it anyway. Stuffing the sausage in his mouth, he let out a little moan, barely audible. Mia gestured for it to be louder, waving her arms around like a lunatic. He shoved it deeper in his mouth, moaning loud enough to make Mia laugh.

Jack's eyes focused on the comments. Between sexual comments and dick jokes, people began to question the laugh, and before he knew it, someone asked, "*Is Mia there??*"

He shook his head without even realizing, moaning louder to cover up Mia's laughter. She covered her mouth, but it was to no avail. Viewers heard her.

Comments streamed in.

"*Bring Mia on!*"

"*Is that a different woman??*"

"*We miss Mia!*"

Before Jack knew it, the number of viewers grew to ten thousand in the first five minutes. He'd never had a stream grow this large so fast.

Mia saw his eyes fixated on the viewer count, the way his whole body froze, sausage still in his mouth. The smile remained fixed on her face.

Looks like I know what I'm doing when it comes to viewership.

Jack realized he was sitting like a statue with a wrinkled sausage in his mouth. He chewed through it, swallowing quickly and taking another bite. The dry meat built up in his throat. His eyes glanced over at the glass of milk, something the viewers couldn't see yet. With a sigh, he reached over, still gripping the meaty hammer in one hand.

His esophagus swelled, the meat clumping in a painful knot. The milk sloshed down his throat, thicker than he thought whole milk should be. Viewers cheered, sending hearts and emojis and comments in the thousands. Jack watched over the glass, gulping it down to force the meat into his stomach.

This is going to be the best stream yet. And it wasn't even my idea.

Jack set down the glass of milk, feeling it wash the meat from his esophagus and fill his gut. He removed the meatballs from the sausage, plucking free the toothpicks and flicking them aside. In one bite, he stuffed in a whole meatball, watching as Mia kept herself from laughing. She covered her mouth with a hand, her eyes red and bulging from the effort of containing her laughter.

Jack's cheeks puffed out, shining in the ring light. He chewed cautiously, trying to keep the ground meat from raining down from his lips and onto his chest. The meatballs were dry and flavorless, as if all the fat from them had been sucked away.

Mia watched him, pinching her leg to help keep from laughing. Seven minutes into the stream, and she shook her head, wondering how many people were watching. Her phone buzzed in her back pocket, and she realized she could join herself and see.

One-hundred-thirty-two thousand.

Mia gasped. Viewers were sending hearts and emojis like crazy, each emoji earning them a few dollars.

Jack looked at the screen, squinting to see the number. The meat froze in his throat halfway down.

I can't believe it. I've never reached a hundred thousand before.

He went to breathe, a crumble of dry meat lodging in his windpipe. Jack croaked, his eyes widening. Throwing the meat in his hand across the room, he reached for his throat, and coughed, spraying ground beef across the trays of sausages. A piece hit Mia in the temple, finally drawing her attention away from the rancid comment section.

She stood frozen, watching him hack. Would she chance getting in front of the camera? It had always been a rule of Jack's that she remained behind the lens at all times, and did she really want to be associated with this video?

She decided *no*.

Jack's eyes bugged from his reddening face, and he wondered if he would ever get the air back in his lungs. Panic and elation spread across the viewers.

"*What's going on?*"

"*Is this real??*"

"*Oh, nice! Fatass is gonna die on camera for us!*"

Mia looked on, confused. Although she had aimed a gun at his head earlier in the day, she had not been prepared to watch him die. Now watching him choke on dry meat, she was indifferent as to whether or not he would ever breathe again. She no longer saw the man she had married within the trembling blob in front of her. In fact, she thought of a life where she was single and the star of her own show. She would use the money from Jack's channels, deleting them forever, and record her own travel vlogs where she would tour the finest boutiques. It had been her dream since she started vlogging, something she was so close to doing with Jack. He would allow her time to look around these boutiques, but never let her buy.

Yes, she watched him gasp for air, clawing at his throat. The end of all her worries was near.

Jack felt the crumble move further down his trachea, inching closer to his lungs. Once inside, what would it do? Would it collapse one of his lungs, or would he be able to breathe again only to have a severe infection inevitably kill him? He had no time to think about those things. He only had enough oxygen in his brain to think about removing the clump and how Mia stood watching him, stone cold.

In a last-ditch effort, Jack shoved his index finger into his mouth. His fingernail tickled his uvula, and he felt his stomach clench. He forced it further, feeling the milky meat rise from his turbulent gut.

Mia stumbled backward as a wave of thick, white liquid flew from Jack's lips. The sound made her squirm, and she scurried across the room.

The milk with meat chunks managed to cover the entire table, sloshing over the sides and soaking deep into the carpet. A sickly acidic smell filled the air, alongside Jack's sour BO. Jack gasped, his airway finally cleared. He sat, stunned and embarrassed. The camera still rolled.

After live streams air, they usually automatically post. Would this be something Jack wanted stuck on his page? As the viewer count hit two-hundred thousand, he supposed so.

Sacrifices will have to be made.

He finally felt the high of recording. Hundreds of thousands of eyes were on him in this moment. The star of the show decided *the show must go on.* He reached for another sausage, to Mia's utter surprise, and gobbled it down, barely missing the toothpicks. It tasted like rotten milk and bile, but it slid down his throat with ease.

Viewership climbed as people sent friends and family and coworkers messages about this idiot vomiting on camera. Even as the traditional ASMR fans left the stream, fans of all things disgusting flooded in.

There he is.

She sat at her desk at work, the live stream taking up most of her desktop screen. He had just vomited, and she could feel nothing but love for him. To be able to care for him was all she could ever ask for. To touch his skin and cook for him would be ecstasy.

Her apartment would be the only one to greet her when she got home, and she was one of the few working in the office since Covid.

Should I do it?

Talk of Mia in the comments worried her. Was she still part of the picture? If so, did she read his messages?

Just saying hi won't hurt.

After the last live stream, she had lost all courage to DM him. She believed he'd never want to talk to her.

Maybe he thinks I'm a weirdo. I mean, my profile picture is him.

Sounds of Jack chewing another meatball filled her ears. Her headphones kept the sounds from escaping into the rest of the office. She sighed and smiled.

The worst he can do is say nothing.

Pulling out her phone, she unlocked it, the lock screen being a photo of Jack in his early days, before he had gained a little over two hundred pounds. Her passcode was 2-0-1-1, the year Jack started making videos with Mia, and the year she had first laid eyes on Jack. Almost a decade of watching this man. She'd seen him scuba dive, sky dive, shoot a cannon, and now she watched him sensually eat at least two times a day. Plus, she was sure to always watch his shorter videos as soon as they came out. A favorite of hers was his unboxing videos. She'd considered sending him a gift, but what do you send to someone who's been all over the world?

"*Hi,*" she typed. Just as quickly, she erased it. "*How are you?*" She shook her head. "*Nice to finally talk to you.*" She chewed her thumbnail, unsure what to say.

"Rochelle?" her boss said, standing next to her desk. He couldn't see either of her screens from where he stood, but he saw the anguish on her face.

Rochelle looked up quickly, removing her headphones. "Uh, yes, sir?" She slid the hand not holding her phone over to her mouse and minimized the window as quietly as possible.

He smiled. "Just thought I'd let you know I'm heading out to dinner at Jones' Dive tonight." He paused, shuffling his feet. Johnson kept his gray hair gelled upward like he was perpetually full of static electricity, and he told everyone his first name was Johnson. According to him, his last name was David, confusing everyone he introduced himself to.

Johnson David stood before Rochelle and said, "I was curious if you'd like to come with?"

Rochelle looked over this man's rumpled dress shirt, which lay wrinkled over his slight beer belly. The lilac color did not do his flushed skin any favors, and the way in which it was pulled out of his cargo pants was unflattering. She could smell the cheap cologne from where she sat and saw the sweat stains under his arms, which were sure to smell of stagnant, sour men's deodorant.

Her hesitation caused the smile on his face to falter, but when she said, "Yes," it regained its place.

"Awesome!" He dialed himself back quickly. "Uh, I can drive you over there straight from here if you'd like."

Rochelle shook her head. "That's okay. I'll meet you there."

"Okay." Johnson left her after tapping her desk lightly, a wide grin on his face.

If it hadn't been for her empty fridge at home, she wouldn't have agreed.

The chat with Jack was still open on her phone, and with a sigh, she closed it. She slipped her headphones back on and opened the live stream's window.

Jack held a meatball in the palm of his hand and said, "Want to see a magic trick?" Then he made it disappear between his lips and chewed with no trace of fear in his eyes.

Rochelle watched, entranced by this man. She'd always loved to cook, and having boyfriends in the past who didn't appreciate her food, she'd kill to have a man eat every bite.

He could swallow up half a cow in one sitting.

"Geez, you're not watching that *weirdo*, are you?" Ricky, the janitor, asked from behind her.

Rochelle jumped, throwing her headphones off, closing the tab, and hitting her knee on her desk all within three seconds. She turned around to meet Ricky's wide eyes.

"*Oh,* so that's how it is." He smirked and walked away, leaving Rochelle with absolutely no words to say.

One more meatball, Jack.

Mia watched in awe.

After vomiting, Jack had managed to pack away five sausages, seven meatballs, and three glasses of milk. Mia was opening the second jug, staring at Jack with her mouth agape, when she remembered her original plan. She quickly checked the views, seeing they had racked up to 353,000. Mia shook her head, certain they weren't ready for what was about to happen.

A special plate of sausages had been prepared and set aside behind the camera. It only held three sausages, but these sausages were *special*. Mia had taken the rod from a rotisserie and hollowed out the center of each of these schlongs. She placed the turkey baster she had set alongside them into the jug of milk and sucked up a good amount. Out of the corner of her eye, she could see Jack focusing on staring at the tip of the sausage he was about to eat, trying to make a show out of gorging on it. She'd always wondered why he chose to sexualize his shows, but now it only played in her favor.

Mia lodged the tip of the turkey baster into the sausage, thrusting it deep into the meat until it remained three-quarters of the way in. Holding this monstrosity behind her back like a killer doll would hold a knife, Mia stood beside Jack, just out of view of the camera. She watched the screen, letting the tip of the sausage in front of the camera, slowly inching toward the side of Jack's face. Jack, busy licking a sausage, didn't happen to look. Mia wondered if he knew something was coming but didn't want to let on to viewers.

As Jack stuck a sausage between his lips, Mia squeezed the turkey baster, squirting him in the side of the head with milk. It dripped down his cheek, slithering down his lips and chin and soaking his chest.

Mia held her breath, pulling the sausage away and backing up. She waited for a reaction. Maybe anger or a play into the sexual relationship this man had with his food, but—

There was nothing. He licked his lips in a non-sensual way and continued to chomp on the sausage in his hands.

Mia checked the stream, seeing it had jumped to four-hundred thousand. Comments rolled in, hearts fluttered across the screen, and best of all, people sent in emojis by the hundreds.

A pit formed in her gut. She had expected this to be torture for Jack, but watching him, he seemed to be just as content as usual. Watching viewers call her husband a hog and a beast, Mia sighed.

He's happy because of all the views you got him.

Yeah, but I just humiliated him on camera in front of hundreds of thousands of people.

Any publicity is good, even if it's bad.

She knew this little voice in her head was right, and that's when she remembered a cabinet in the kitchen, one up so high she had to get on a stool to get to it, ensuring Jack could never reach it. A cabinet full of boxes and parcels, each labeled with badly written notes to *Jack of Jack Eats the Box.*

The stream ended at five-hundred thousand, earning Jack's channel an award as well as ten-thousand dollars.

"Ten-thousand dollars!" they both shouted together. Even through all her frustration, Mia hugged Jack, and Jack allowed it. They scrolled through the donations together, sure to write down everyone's names to send out special thank yous.

Jack shook his head. "Record-breaking."

Mia rolled her eyes, still writing down donors' names. "Maybe for us."

"Yeah, but ten Gs." Jack felt excitement brewing in him. He was growing as a digital creator, but looking over at Mia, he knew it wasn't all his doing. He was frustrated, unsure whether to thank her or slap her for making a pork sausage jizz on him.

Does it really matter?

"Thank you, Mia," he said.

Mia's eyes widened, and she looked away from her list. Jack looked her in her eyes, a smile on his face. In her mind, she raced back seven years to a night in Cairo. She'd picked out a restaurant for them to go to—the best meal Jack had ever had, according to him. He thanked her that night. Thanked her for the lovely meal, for being there with him, and for being his wife.

Rage filled her.

What is he pulling?

It had been months, maybe even years, since he said thank you.

Now that his channel is doing good, he wants to kiss my ass? Yeah, fucker.

She wanted to spit in his face, to scream at him, tell him how much she wished he was dead, but something in his eyes prevented her from doing so.

He's falling for me again. That void inside of him is filling all because of this stupid stream, leaving him enough attention to give me a bite, but soon, very soon, that void will reopen, and who will bear the brunt of it all?

The voice in the back of her mind whispered, *You will, dear.*

Jack lay in bed, freshly bathed, with clean sheets and a clean bedroom floor. The fan was on high, cooling his feverish skin. He'd even asked Mia to open the windows, letting in the refreshing mountain mist that resided around their home, and letting out the foul, rank air that accumulated from three years of Jack's strange existence.

He lay on his back, staring at the ceiling as he always did. His side throbbed, that rib sitting in his flesh uncomfortably. Jack imagined it was broken, sharp jagged bits of bone able to swim around under his skin, jabbing at him here and there. As he breathed, he saw in his mind the broken rib expanding as his lungs filled with air and stabbing outward, then contracting with his lungs as air left his body, poking inward, nearly missing his lungs. The image made him squirm, causing another slicing pain up his side.

When Mia had gotten Jack into bed, he talked to her softly, going over ways they could make more money with his channel. He had been sleepy and simply rambling with leftover excitement from the day, yet she seemed distant, only nodding her head along with his words. He had even tested her by halting mid-sentence, and she continued nodding her head.

Jack couldn't help but wonder, *What did I do wrong?*

Meanwhile, Mia could only think of all the ways Jack used her. She was listing off ways in her head as he spoke, going through the motions of their nightly routine.

Get him into bed, tuck in the blankets around him in that stupid way he likes, strap on his CPAP and turn it on, plug in his chair to charge, set his phone close enough by him so he can scroll until his heart brings him close enough to death that he sleeps, make sure the fan is on high and the humidifier is on.

And when he asked her to open the windows, she silently cursed him for interrupting her rhythm and thoughts. She had just reached year two in their relationship for ways he had used her. She had been a pawn in his life ever since they met. He'd used her to get into nightclubs and restaurants he'd *never* get into without her.

She'd used him for plenty of things as well, she knew, but when years of a marriage that was a partnership turned completely one-sided, Mia felt she had a right to be angry.

As Jack lay in bed, running over the live stream and wondering how he could improve his channel, Mia showered in the downstairs bathroom. Her clothes were set out on the coffee table, having been washed since the last time they were in her bedroom—her *old* bedroom. She'd noticed an odd smell from all her clothing, and realized with a bout of nausea that Jack was stinking up everything in the house, including her clothes.

Under steaming hot water, Mia took her loofah and vigorously scrubbed at her skin. The friction burned more than the water, and her skin popped a bright red, but it wasn't enough. She inhaled water through her nose by cupping her hands and snorting it, then blew it back out. The smell of rotten ramen and sweat encapsulated her—the same smell embedded within her clothing, the walls, the couch, the pillow she slept on, *her husband.*

She could see him lying in bed as she showered, always imagining him as a plump dumpling with arms and legs, stinking steam rising in tendrils from his slick body. The tendrils had found their way to her nostrils, and there they penetrated and impregnated her senses with their foul aroma.

Mia continued to scrub her body, finally breaking skin and catching sight of blood before rinsing off and hopping out.

The sun had set early for these mountaineers. The pine trees shrouded their home in shadows throughout the day and the sun was always late arriving and early to leave. Jack listened to the fan spin in circles above his body. The mount rocking back and forth created a rhythmic ticking. He listened carefully, just as he did every night, and was close to falling asleep when he realized he was back at his table under the scrutinizing light of the camera stand he had bought when he first started *Jack Eats the Box.*

A silver platter with a matching lid sat before him, the smell of whatever was underneath tantalizing his tongue. The lid floated up and out of his view, to his amazement, and looking down at the platter, he saw it presented a whole roasted turkey to him. His hands reached for it before he even knew what he was doing.

He pinched at the skin, plucking a small piece and setting it on his tongue. Charred butteriness melted over his taste buds like a warm blanket. Jack poked at the now revealed white meat, digging his fingers in and pulling out a chunk.

Something moved in front of him, and he looked up, seeing himself reflected in his phone screen. Hearts and emojis were flooding in. Jack smiled and reached for the leg of the turkey when something came out of the phone.

A hand, darker than black, absorbing all light, reached for him. Jack froze, his fingers in his mouth. The hand gripped the turkey, ripping it from his left hand. It flipped the browned body over, revealing it to be Mia.

She had been cooked 'til her skin peeled off in crispy, flavorful bits, and her meat was juicy and tender. Jack wondered how she'd gotten so small and who'd cooked her. Even through the rich flavor in his mouth, Jack could taste bile. It ran up his throat, a pit of writhing worms in his gut sending it upward.

"*Eat it*," something whispered.

Jack's breath caught in his throat.

"*Eat it. Eat it. Eat it*," voices chanted from behind the screen.

Fat oozed from slits in her skin.

I bet it tastes like gold.

"*Eat it. Eat it. Eat it.*"

Jack breathed again, letting out a heavy, pent-up breath, and grabbed Mia's ankle. It was crispy, and her foot was charred black, the toenails curled backward. He rested a hand on her exposed breasts—had she had more meat there, he would have started with those—and violently twisted the ankle. He heard her hip pop out of place and the tendon rip. Meat hung loosely around her thigh as he held up her leg.

"*Eat it. Eat it. Eat it.*"

Slowly, Jack inched the meat closer to his mouth, the smell of her cooked thigh making his tongue wet. He pulled his lips and jaws apart, setting the tender leg in his mouth. His teeth sunk in spurting juices onto his chin. His eyes rolled back, the flavor divine.

Mia screamed.

From within her burnt, small head, a wail escaped into the room. The black hand seemed to reach for her, the voices still chanting behind it, when it suddenly took hold of Mia's leg, snatching it from Jack's hand. His mouth full of meat, the hand shoved the leg, foot first, into Jack's mouth. Jack gagged.

"*Eat it. Eat it. Eat it.*"

Mia's toes wriggled around in the back of his throat as the hand shoved her leg further in. Her screams bellowed through the room, piercing his ears. The taste of burnt, black death filled his mouth. The hand reared back, and with an open palm, it smacked the end of Mia's thigh, sending her foot through the back of Jack's neck.

Jack gasped, and he was staring up at the ceiling in his bedroom. The night air filtered in through his windows as he panted.

Mia sat on the couch, a quart of peppermint ice cream on her lap.

When did they sell this stuff? Isn't it only in December? This stuff's got to be almost a year old.

All the while she wondered that, she stuffed spoonfuls into her mouth. It was rare for her to break her diet, something drilled into her since her young pageant days. It wasn't hard for her to eat clean. It was hard for her to keep any food in the house that wasn't garbage. That issue only presented itself within the last three years since Jack started his own channel.

Mia swore she went over these details every night, repeatedly until her eyelids would finally close, temporarily shutting down the thoughts. The doctor said it was insomnia. She believed it was stress—just something that would go away once the problem was solved.

How many times have I begged Jack to stop? How many times have I begged him to go to the doctor?

The last time Jack went for a check-up was almost at that three-year mark. Even when he broke his leg, he refused to be weighed or have his blood pressure checked. Mia had gone along to the last check-up as she always did. Jack couldn't remember what medications he was taking, so she would talk to the doctor. After being weighed, the nurse wrote down Jack's weight, and when the doctor checked his charts, she looked at him questioningly.

"What's changed in your life, Jack?" she had asked.

"What do you mean?" Jack asked in return.

Mia dreaded the question, already noticing the decline in Jack's health. The pallor of his skin lacked the vitality it used to have. His skin sagged in places it didn't use to, especially around his mouth. He had started off doing mukbang videos with fruits and vegetables and healthy options, but when he began taking people's suggestions, all they would suggest was junk food and fast food. His most common video, and most asked for, was trying items from a fast-food chain called Grizzly's. They specialized in sloppy barbecue, their most popular item being their beef-pork-bison burger, which also included a helping of onion rings, french fries, and bacon on top of the patty and a small bucket of mayonnaise mixed with ranch to go with. The entire thing from bun to bun was slathered in barbecue sauce, and people loved it. Mia couldn't touch a thing from Grizzly's.

The doctor had looked at Mia, noticing she was staring at the floor. Mia could feel the doctor's eyes on her. The appointment had ended abruptly when Jack stood up and stated they had somewhere to go. The doctor had just gotten into the room and argued she'd like to do a better check-up on him. Jack stormed out of the office, not even waiting for Mia. Mia looked at the doctor helplessly, and the woman said, "If he doesn't change his habits, he's going to gain weight rapidly. I don't know much about his family history, but if heart problems are common in his family, he could die."

Mia stuffed another big spoonful of peppermint ice cream into her mouth, savoring the texture, one she had so little a chance to enjoy.

What if I made mukbang videos?

She smirked, sure she would get double the subscribers Jack had in much less time. Then again, she didn't want to be three-hundred pounds.

She licked the spoon, secretly trying to do so sensually just like Jack. Giggling, she shook her head.

I guess it's just not my thing.

The clock next to her read one o' nine. Nothing but the green glow of said clock and the soft moonlight accompanied her. These late nights and early mornings were hers—the only thing that *was* hers besides the lower floor of the house.

And the car and the outside world.

Mia's face scrunched, her usually smooth skin wrinkling.

No, don't do that to me. It's his fault he's that big. It's his fault he broke his leg coming down the stairs.

That small voice in the back of her head dreadfully whispered, *You cook. You clean. You bathe him. You've changed the furniture to fit his body. You bought him a CPAP. You've given suggestions for videos and helped him record.*

You're an enabler.

She felt her mood sink. The peppermint ice cream no longer tasted minty. It slid across her tongue like cold slush. Her throat tensed as a fresh onslaught of tears fought their way to the surface. She set the spoon into the carton and covered her mouth just in time to stifle a sob.

So, what do we do from here?

There was a pause, and for a moment, Mia knew she was crazy. Listening to a voice in her head like it was another person was an insane idea to her, yet, it made her feel better. It made her feel like someone else understood the situation.

Her mother hadn't been in contact since that night Mia called her. She felt Roxanne was too ashamed to talk to her. It made her feel hollow and alone. Then there it was, that little voice speaking to her, giving her its wisdom.

We force him to the edge of death and let him decide.

Shortly after his nightmare, there had been a *ding*. He thought he had turned his phone on silent like every other night, but the notification piqued his curiosity. Jack reached over, the weight of his arm almost too much to move, and felt around for his phone in the dark.

Another message asking me to be an "ambassador" for a brand? he thought, rolling his eyes.

His fingers finally felt the boxiness of his phone, and he slid it over to him. Picking it up, the screen lit up, showing his lock screen:

A photo of him eating a burger from Grizzly's.

He tapped his passcode in, 2-0-1-9, not the year he and his wife were married, but the year he had started his own channel. He tapped the most recent message.

User *iheartjack* had messaged.

Jack's heart throbbed in his chest.

He read the message so quickly he had to reread it two times before finally comprehending what it said.

Good evening, Jack.

Followed by a black heart emoji.

Are black hearts a good thing?

Jack sat, unsure what to say.

Hi, he typed.

Then he erased it.

Hey.

Followed by four backspaces.

What do you even say to a girl as beautiful as her? And more importantly, what does she want from me?

Five minutes had passed since she sent the message as Jack thought over what he should say.

She's going to think I'm ignoring her.

In haste, Jack sent:

Ho!

Reading over his sent message, Jack's eyes widened to the size of eggs. He scrambled to unsend the message, but she had already seen it.

I meant hi! I'm so sorry. I'm really sorry, he typed quickly. She saw this message as well and began typing. Shortly after, a laughing emoji appeared.

No worries! she said.

Jack waited, watching the three dots bounce up and down as she typed.

How are you? she asked.

How am I? he thought.

I'm good. Hbu? he sent.

Butterflies fluttered around in his stomach, carrying away his grogginess and the memories of his nightmare.

Good :) what are you doing awake? she said. *It's late here in California.*

Jack's eyes widened. *California?*

He typed quickly, asking what part of California she was from before erasing it. *Way too forward.* He opted to say he was just staring at the ceiling and that it *is* late here in California.

You're from California, too?! she asked.

Jack wondered how close the two might be. And the conversation went as such:

Jack: *I am. So, what are you doing up so late?*

iheartjack: *oh…I just got back from this really awful date [teary face]*

Jack: *aww I'm sorry. Can I ask, what happened?*

iheartjack: *of course you can. So my boss asked me out to dinner coz I was working late*

Jack: *[cringe emoji]*

iheartjack: *right? Anyway, I said yeah coz the guy is nice and tbh a girl could eat*

Jack: *uh huh*

iheartjack: *I expected maybe a small burger joint or something but no he takes me to a divey bar/restaurant with games inside*

Jack: *a casino?*

iheartjack: *no like kid's games*

Jack: *oh*

iheartjack: *yeah like arcade games but instead of screaming kids there was like biker gang members and drug dealers playing*

Jack: *wow sounds scary*

iheartjack: *I know! And we sit down across from this old couple who keeps looking at us—I am like fifteen years younger than my boss*

Jack: *oof*

iheartjack: *yeah, but I didn't want to like kiss him or anything*

Jack: *mmhmm*

iheartjack: *I didn't!!!*

Jack: *okay*

iheartjack: *anyway [eye roll emoji] finally the old people get up to leave but on their way out, the old man says "you have a lovely daughter, sir, she looks just like you!"*

Jack: *no way!*

iheartjack: *yes way! And my boss is like hella white. Got blue eyes and everything. Meanwhile, I'm clearly Mexican. I think dude just did it to fuck with my boss [laughing emoji]*

Jack: *[three laughing emojis]*

iheartjack: *So that made it SUPER awkward even tho it was already weird. And you know what made it worse?*

Jack: *what?*

iheartjack: *he ordered clams...*

Jack: *okay?*

iheartjack: *AND EVERY TIME HE ATE ONE, HE HAD TO LICK BETWEEN THE SHELL FIRST*

Jack: *NO WAY*

iheartjack: *YES WAY*

Jack: *that's disgusting!*

iheartjack: *and he did it while talking, while making eye contact, even touched my shoe with his shoe when tonguing one of them down*

Here Jack made a mental note to order clams for one of his videos. He'd never liked seafood, but he could see his fans going crazy for it.

Jack: *did you leave?*

iheartjack: *No! He's my boss! I don't wanna get fired.*

Jack's eyes grew weary. He wanted to sleep, but this woman had finally talked to him privately. Although he desperately yearned to talk to her on the phone, to hear her voice and bond, he knew his CPAP machine would hiss in the background. Not to mention, he couldn't imagine what Mia would do.

Mia. That psycho bitch.

He shook his head, mulling over his options. Mia checked his emails but not his DMs, and she was out of the picture on camera, so maybe this *iheartjack* would believe him if he said he's single.

Maybe I can keep Mia while she's good for the work until this one is ready for me.

Jack: *Was that all he did?*

iheartjack: *I wish! He got so stinking drunk that he slipped up and told me I remind him of his nanny from childhood [crying emoji]*

Jack: *Omg that's terrible!*

iheartjack: *I know!! Why is it always me???*

Jack: *what do you mean?*

iheartjack: *I can never find a nice guy to treat me right. I mean, I had to sneak out because he fell asleep at the table*

Jack felt tremendously sorry for the girl.

With good looks like hers, she should be marrying a prince.

Mia had pulled out her laptop, researching *the top ten most unhealthy foods* and *recipes to make your arteries solid*. Most of the foods that came up were fried and full of fat. She even stumbled across a few videos of people eating stuff like fried butter in nacho cheese and mayonnaise on pizza.

Disgusting, she thought, a smirk on her face.

She wondered if the woman who delivered their groceries would notice a change in their habitual products. Mia ordered groceries weekly, generally needing to restock the ramen, milk, ice cream, her food, and a few bulk meals like spaghetti and bread or, like this last video, sausages and meatballs. Everything else was ordered via restaurant delivery or food shipment companies, like the company in Japan that Jack ordered his marshmallows from every month.

This coming week's order was bound to be full of oils, butter, mayonnaise, frozen pizzas, ice cream, and all the frozen, fried foods Jack could eat. Extra potato chips. Extra candy. Extra soda. Extra. Extra. *Extra.*

Mia was sure she was going to start ordering from Grizzly's two times more than she had been, finally appeasing Jack's wants. And she would be sure to get those boxes down from that high up cabinet.

Chapter Four: Notes of Chocolate and Death

"*Hey guys!* Today we'll be opening a box from User *1800getlaid*," Jack said from his table, which held a haphazardly taped parcel. Mia watched the screen, ensuring he was within the frame. Unlike his live streams, his regular videos were recorded in landscape with the back camera and edited later on by a man they met in England years prior.

"This one slipped past me, so it's a couple months old. But I appreciate your kind gift."

Mia cringed at his baby voice.

Pudgy fingers prodded at the package, short fingernails searching for a place to peel the tape.

Jack's mind seemed to be elsewhere as he scratched at the cardboard. *iheartjack* had talked to him until he fell asleep for the past few days. The last thing he remembered from their chat the night before was a sleepy selfie from her. Her image glowed in his mind—his online goddess.

"*Jack*," Mia snapped. "You need a knife?"

He looked up at her, glaring. "Yes, preferably to slit my throat." His large fingers unfurled at her, gesturing to put a knife in his hand.

Mia rolled her eyes. "I can see the gravy pouring from the slash now." She handed him a box cutter she had in her pocket.

"Haha, yeah, funny." Jack set the knife off to the side of the camera view, steadying his body and face once again, before reaching for the knife.

Mia shook her head, sure the editor would have a lot of questions.

He slipped the blade through the tape, a pungent odor breaking out into the room. His face contorted, an attempt to push the smell from his nostrils. Mia raised an eyebrow before the smell hit her.

She had been passive aggressively hiding packages from Jack. He *loved* getting presents, but usually she went through the boxes first. Her cabinet of gifts could be full of *anything*. This one smelled as if it were full of rotten pig heads.

Even with this image in her mind, Mia was not prepared for what Jack pulled from the box.

Thinking it had to be a gag, Jack grabbed the thing barehanded, instantly regretting his decision. Slowly, he revealed to the camera the decomposed body of an iguana. With his other hand, he moved the box aside, and a note fluttered down from the iguana's body, having been stuck to its feet.

Refraining from gagging, Jack picked up the note. It had been stained with juices from the body, assuming it was fresh when it had been so carefully packed and shipped.

Reading the note aloud, Jack said, "*Dear Jack, here is my pet iguana Lime-Ade. He liked to eat cilantro and bite before he got in a fight with the wrong dog. I love watching your channel, and Lime-Ade used to watch with me. I think he would love to be immortalized through one of your videos.*" Jack's eyes ran down the page, getting to, "*P.S. I want you to eat him with his favorite food: cilantro.*"

Jack stared at the camera, dumbfounded. Mia stared at him, equally dumbfounded, yet a grin spread across her lips. She shook her head, fighting off her bubbling laughter.

"*Well,*" Jack abruptly said, looking up to Mia. She shrugged her shoulders, and he resented the smug smirk on her face. He gazed back into the camera. "I don't think I'll be eating this kind contribution to my channel, but I appreciate the sentiment."

Mia waited a second, knowing the editor would be pissed to deal with her barging in too soon. "You should leave that thing on the table as you open the other boxes."

Jack shook his head, setting the iguana back in the box. "There's no way."

"*You have to.*"

Her sudden tone shift made Jack look at her. "*Why?*"

"Because this kid sent in his pet to be immortalized and all you did was unbox him and disappoint the kid by saying no."

Jack scoffed, pushing the box as far away from himself as possible. "I'm *not* doing that." He crossed his arms.

Mia crossed hers in imitation. "Then I'm *not* helping with the rest of the video, and *you* can just wheel yourself around the second floor while *I* go on about my day."

Jack narrowed his eyes on her. They were already running behind. The editor would need at least two hours to edit the file, thumbnail, and description, and Jack's schedule bore down on him.

"*Fine.*" He snatched the box and pulled out the iguana. Out of anger, he gripped the body too hard, his fingers squishing through its skin. Something wet tickled the tips of his fingers. He set the thing down, and asked, "Is it in the camera?"

Mia saw the revulsion on his face, and even with the iguana in perfect view of the camera without obstructing the view of Jack, she told him to scoot it over to the left.

He did so.

"You know what? Move it back, it looked better than before. Yeah, just, oh, too far." She bent down, looking at the screen and hiding her smile behind it. "Oh, right—damn too far to the left. Just a little this way. Ah, no, not there. Just uh—"

"*God damn it, Mia. You do it!*"

"Oh, oh, it's fine," she said, laughing.

The smell entered their noses and settled in, making each of them equally queasy. Mia reached down to the pile of boxes and envelopes on the floor, thinking of what Jack said as he saw them all. *Those all came today?* She had laughed and confessed she didn't feel like going through them all, so she'd hidden them away. He'd been upset, but appeased when she offered her thoughts on how it could improve his viewership. His scheduled videos were usually monologues, involving him talking into the camera about how his travels affected his pallet and his thoughts on food. Mia didn't think anyone took Jack's opinions on food seriously and was damn sure viewers would be more interested in unboxing videos.

Grabbing one, she wondered what was inside, and the image of several months old, severed fingers jumbling around within the bubble wrap lining the paper envelope flooded her mind.

Needless to say, she was disappointed when Jack pulled out two chocolate bars. A note included in the package stated the sender had spent the summer in Germany as a foreign exchange student and had picked out these bars for him. Mia recognized the brand as the most commonly sold chocolate bar in all of Germany. She and Jack had gorged themselves on the bars the first week of their stay in Berlin, having found them at every small and large shop around the town.

"*Oooh, I love these!*" he squealed.

Mia squirmed, leaving the room. She figured Jack could remain in the same spot as he ate the chocolate bars. With only about five minutes, Mia raced down the stairs to check the day's progress. Ever since his sausage video a week ago, she'd been keeping a follow/view/likes log. A chart labeled with each type of video Jack did awaited her. It had been twenty-four hours since she'd posted his last image post, and the time to check its stats on each platform had almost run past her.

Jack smiled at the camera, his skin shining in the light and the taste of the iguana's decay heavy in the back of his throat. He peeled open one of the chocolates, looking up. The grin hurt his cheeks.

I don't want to do this right now.

Chunks of almond protruded from the bar, looking like toenails. A bitter taste filled his mouth, slicking over his tongue. Jack's attention shifted to the iguana, its black, shriveled eyes staring at him.

Jack took a large bite. Chocolate melted on his tongue, a flavor he would have enjoyed had it not been accompanied by the foul taste of death. Looking at the camera, he chewed through the almond bits with the image of iguana spines crunching between his teeth strong in his mind. Although trying not to cringe, Jack failed.

He thought his words might cover up his discomfort and said, "*Mmm, delicious.*" His voice quavered and cracked, a small crumble of chocolate tumbling out of his mouth. It bounced off his left boob and landed on the floor. Jack looked down at it, his appetite diminished to nothing. Only a swirling pit of nausea took up the space in his abdomen.

"*Mia!*" Tears streamed down his face. "*Meeee-uuuuuuh!*" he wailed, like a child lost at an amusement park.

Having been at her computer in the family room, Mia pushed her chair back and rushed upstairs. She could hear the tears in his voice.

"What is it?" she asked, panting.

"Mia," he said, his eyes and face red and wet. He shook his head, his waddle wobbling. "*I don't want to do this anymore.*"

Mia shook her head fervently. "What do you mean?"

"I—I can't get out of this chair, Mia. When my ass scratches, I just have to pretend it doesn't because I can't stand up to scratch it. Shit, I probably couldn't reach it if I could get up." He threw his hands out, sobbing. "I—I haven't walked in—in months. What am I—what am I even doing?"

Mia stood in stunned silence.

"Like who am I?" He slung his index finger toward the dead iguana. "Who do people think I—I am if they're sending me dead things to eat?"

Mia looked at the iguana and back to her husband. It was rare that she saw him cry. The last time had most likely been four years prior, when his dog was put down. He had stood beside his best friend, petting her and whispering encouraging things to the almost comatose dog. The gray of her fur spread throughout her face, and the vet had told him the cancer was terminal. Jack embraced Sandy, his dog of fifteen years, and let the vet inject poison into her. Mia watched, never having seen him so emotional. He looked up to the ceiling as Sandy relaxed against him, and he screamed, asking God why.

Even at his own mother's funeral, he had remained stone cold under his mask. Teary eyes over medical masks floated about the hall that Sandra's funeral was held in, all except Jack's. His eyes remained dry, his nose without a sniffle.

"*Nothing to say now?*" he snapped.

Mia recognized this tone at least. "No, not really." She pulled up a chair across the table from him and shut off the camera and lights. Sitting down and looking deep into his eyes, she started with, "You've built a huge following and a community of people who love you." She took a deep breath, regretting it. Between the iguana and Jack, she couldn't tell who stunk worse. "Why would you give all that up?"

Jack mulled this over, looking away for a moment. "It was you that said I'm '*committing suicide by butter.*' Why the sudden change of heart?"

Mia spoke quickly, the little voice in the back of her head saying, *You're going to let him quit? After all you've endured?* "Because you said this is all you have. What will you have if you quit?"

"Well, I'll have you." Jack also thought of a certain young woman in southern California.

Nothing but silence met his words, and Jack's mood shifted as he realized what the silence meant.

"*You'd leave me if I lost my following?!*"

She threw up her hands. "I didn't say *that*."

"You didn't have to!" Jack's cheeks had dried and flushed red.

"Well, what else do I get from this relationship?"

Jack thought about her comment about him not initiating sex in months and sighed.

Money. She sticks around for the money.

He wanted to say something that would hurt her, something that would sting.

"*I wouldn't have sex with you even if I was the same size I was when we got together.*"

Mia felt ashamed of how much the statement stung. She held back tears, bolting out the door and down the stairs. Grabbing her keys, she headed for the front door before realizing she had nowhere to go in this state beside the house. Her mother and father resided thousands of miles away, and an empty hotel room sounded about as good as a punch in the gut.

She was alone.

Chapter Five: Separating the Yolk

She packed her things and slowly added boxes and suitcases by the front door.

Jack hadn't noticed between his healthy mukbang streams and his new exercise videos. These new videos showed him sitting in his chair, no table in front of him. From his head to his feet took up the entire screen. He liked to wave his arms around in circles or attempt to lift his legs. No music. No inspirational soundtrack. No speaking. Only the sound of his skin pulling away from the vinyl of his seat and his heavy breathing.

Viewership had gone down tremendously, and Jack pretended he didn't care, but it ate away at him, much like his stomach did every night.

First it was the cravings.

For the first live stream in what Jack hoped would be the change he needed in his life, Mia prepared grilled chicken and watermelon and steamed broccoli in heaping amounts to please his appetite, but even after finishing the meal, he found himself hungry. It wasn't the usual stomach growling and empty feeling, but his brain told him he was still hungry, despite his gut being full of warm food.

On a trip to Jerusalem, Mia and Jack fasted. Locals told them how it would change their perspective on food; how it would make them appreciate every bite that much more and the meal right after fasting would be the best they'd ever had.

Jack had to agree but didn't make fasting part of his lifestyle. The agony of his stomach crying out all day had been enough to make him an irritable monster, but this feeling was ten times worse. He had eaten just like his body asked, but his brain pretended as if it hadn't happened. It incessantly begged him to eat more. The live stream ended, and there he sat at his table, hollow. His usual high was not there. His usual feeling of completion and satisfaction was gone. He wasn't even comfortably sleepy.

Mia knew he would struggle to stave off the cravings, but she also knew she wouldn't be there for it much longer. The color of Jack's skin returned as her emotions left. She only offered nods and grunts in return for his words.

"You ready to make today's video?" he would ask.

"Mmhmm," she would respond.

Mia went through the motions, stacking away money and bags as she went. She felt incredibly sad that the only people she could turn to in these times were her parents. The day finally came when she was ready. She was packed, she had hired an in-home care nurse to keep Jack alive, using his own credit card of course, and she felt entirely disconnected from Jack and their home in California.

If you think I'd choose you over half a million followers, you're stupid! replayed in her mind day and night. Despite his change in heart and demeanor, it was all she could hear every time he opened his mouth.

And now that he wants to be "healthy" he's not even going to have a platform or money to offer. What's left?

She cried herself to sleep nightly, her heart torn between staying and leaving.

Jack saw her change. He thought she'd be happy. After his first stream with vegetables that weren't fried, he thanked Mia, and she'd had nothing to say.

He went on, thanking her for always being there for him, for taking care of him, for dealing with his *moodiness*. She nodded and left the room, taking the dishes to the kitchen.

Jack's nights were spent talking to Rochelle. He learned a lot about her over the course of a few weeks. She worked for a greeting card company in SoCal. She read the submissions people sent in and sorted them, sending out rejections and acceptances. She lived alone, having moved out of her parents' house at sixteen, and she loved food and cooking.

He thought of her as a good distraction from what he was going through, but deep down he knew he was falling for her. He dreamed of being with her, smelling her, tasting her, as Mia grew more distant every day.

She sat on the couch while he took his afternoon nap.

Today's the day.

Wearing sweatpants and a T-shirt, she wanted to be comfortable for the over forty-hour drive and planned to take breaks only when she couldn't hold her pee or couldn't keep her eyes open. Her tank was full. Surprisingly, her bags and suitcases and boxes all fit into her car, taking up residence in the trunk, the back seat, and the passenger seat. She didn't have as many belongings as she thought. The house looked no emptier than it did when all of her things were neatly tucked away.

Her chest tightened as she waited for the in-home nurse.

I'll wake him up and break the news while the nurse is downstairs. Then I'll slip out while he reacts.

She wondered if he'd yell or cry or even react at all, her knee bouncing.

What if he has a heart atta—

The doorbell rang, making Mia jump. Her heart thudded in her chest as she walked to the door. She imagined opening it to see Jack standing there.

"What are you doing, Mia?" he'd ask.

She'd scream and run upstairs to see his bed and chair empty, and he'd thunder after her, busting the stairs as he went.

Her hand gripped the doorknob, and she twisted it. It creaked open as she peered around it.

A slender man with dark skin smiled at her. His scrubs were a light green that matched his striking eyes. Mia smiled back, at ease.

In a low voice, she said, "Hi, he's upstairs asleep."

"Hi, I'm Deryk." He reached out to shake her hand.

They shook hands, and she let him in. With him, he carried a clipboard and a duffle bag. She showed him to the couch, freshly cleaned of her makeshift bed, and sat down in the chair across from him.

"I guess I should fill you in." She sighed, hands fiddling with themselves in her lap. She'd expected an old woman to show up; someone she could confess this sickening part of her life to. But no, a handsome man of her age showed up, and she was nervous to tell him all the disgusting details.

"You don't have to do anything." He smiled gently. "I'm just here to take care of him."

Tears rushed to her eyes. She pursed her lips to keep the crying at bay and shook her head when she failed. "It's been so *hard*." She covered her face with her hands, wiping the tears away. "I think I just need to get away for a while."

"How long have you been taking care of him?" he asked.

"Well, we used to travel, but—"

"I used to watch your vlogs honestly," he said. Mia thought she could see him blushing, but in the dim gray light from the windows, she wasn't sure.

She smiled. "Yeah. I miss those days."

"I miss seeing you on camera."

Mia's thoughts halted, hung up on his words. "Really?"

"Well, yeah. Now Jack just eats on camera. I can't imagine how you feel. When he made the change, we, well me, but I assume most viewers, too, wondered if you left him, but I guess you just disappeared from the spotlight."

"Yeah."

"Did you see the articles about you?"

"Yeah, yeah, I did." She looked down at her hands. "Jack said it would be best if people thought he was single."

"I mean, yeah, when you want to reach that nasty part of the internet."

Her eyes flicked back up to his. "Nasty part of the internet?"

He laughed. "Yeah, mukbang isn't just ASMR. There's a bunch of perverts out there that get off to that shit. Jack really panders to them, too, sucking on bananas and shit." He shook his head. "I'm happy for him though."

"Oh, yeah?"

"Yeah, it's gotta be rough being that size and making the decision to change. I'll be sure he sticks to it."

Mia mulled over whether she should tell him everything. He was a fan with his own biases about their relationship.

What if he hurts Jack?

So what if he does?

Mia shook her head.

"So, you've been caretaking for him this whole time?"

"Ever since his videos."

"You cook?"

"Mmhmm."

"Clean?"

"Yes."

"And bathe him?"

"Yes, sir."

He shook his head. "You poor woman. How do you help him move around?"

"He's got a system of pulleys and his chair. I'll show you after I let him know."

"He," Deryk stopped, his eyes wide. "He doesn't know yet?"

"No, I didn't feel comfortable telling him with no one else here, and I definitely didn't want to tell him and be stuck living with him and his resentment for a few weeks."

"Can I watch? *I mean*, I'd like to be there in case he tries anything dangerous."

Mia shook her head. "The only thing dangerous he's capable of is eating a heart attack burger from Grizzly's."

Deryk laughed but saw she didn't smirk. He looked at her closer in the small period of silence between their words. Her eyes were circled with purplish skin, indicative that she hadn't been sleeping. He'd always had an affinity for her dark eyes, and when she set them on him, he felt bare in her presence.

"Are you okay?" He kept his voice low and wanted to reach across the space between them to touch her shoulder or her knee—just to break the distance there and connect.

"No, but I guess that's why I'm leaving." She sniveled, shaking her head again. "I just don't see any other option." They stared at each other. "You know what he told me?"

"What?" he asked, on the edge of his seat.

"That he'd take his followers over me." She stood up, throwing her hands outward. "And now this bullshit of trying to get healthier and acting like he's not hurt that he's losing followers. I just *don't understand* what he's doing."

Deryk couldn't understand it either, but he offered what he could. "Maybe he's scared of dying."

Mia thought it over, thinking how she almost blew his head off with the pistol her father had given her. "*Maybe.* Whatever his reasoning may be, I'm leaving."

She walked around the couch, headed for the stairs, when Deryk stood up.

"You stay down here. I'll help you get acquainted with Jack as soon as I'm done. He'll be no harm to me."

Jack slept soundly in his bed, the one he hadn't shared in months with the woman he married. The only woman he had shared it with recently was Rochelle, and she slept in her own bed hundreds of miles away. Their relationship had flourished lately as Mia distanced herself. He found himself confiding in her things he never would have.

Jack: *I've been so horny lately, but I can't do anything about it :(*

Rochelle: *I'm sure I could help with that if we got together ;)*

He longed for her presence, but in a deeper, darker part of himself, he yearned for Mia. Despite their differences, he saw parts of Mia in Rochelle. She was younger and of a different physical appearance, but her kindness brought him back to those early years of marriage.

In his slumber, he was dreaming of a twisted version of reality. He watched Mia gorge herself in front of a camera, and strange voices echoed in the background. In one hand he held a frying pan, and when he looked down into it, he saw mini sausages arranged to spell *DIE*.

Mia gently laid a hand on his shoulder, startling him awake. He opened his eyes to see she was crying, and he reached out his hands to hold her. Pulling away, she shut off his CPAP and helped him take off the mask.

"Jack, I have something I need to tell you."

"I need to tell you something, too." Jack made a firm decision in his mind, giving him the strength to sit up in bed by himself. Mia watched him wriggle up the headboard like a caterpillar out of a hole. She thought she could smell piss, but it wasn't her turn to change his diaper. Jack caught his breath for a second, and as Mia opened her mouth, he spoke first.

"I want to have a baby."

Mia's jaw dropped. After seeing the genuine smile on Jack's face, she held back her laughter, her eyes glistening with tears.

Deryk listened from the bottom of the stairs, covering his mouth with his hand.

"Jack, you know we'd have to have sex to have a baby, right?"

"Well, duh."

"Jack, I'm not having sex with you." The statement came out as cruelly as she hoped it would, preceding the killer. "*I'm leaving you.*"

His face fell slack, like a sack of potatoes off a truck. "You're *what?*"

"I'm leaving back to North Carolina."

Jack's words left his mouth before he could stop them, only after he said them did he realize how wrong they sounded. "Who will take care of me?"

"*Exactly.*" Mia's demeanor went from calm to defensive. "*That's exactly why I'm leaving, Jack. It's always about you.*" She turned toward the door.

Jack's hand shot out, latching on to her wrist. "Mia, *please.*"

Without looking back, she yanked her hand away and stormed through the door. Deryk looked up at her as she barreled down the stairs.

"*I just need a minute*," she said under her breath as she passed him.

She held her phone in her hand, listening to it ring on speaker phone. Leaning against the railing next to their empty hot tub, Mia wiped away tears she was ashamed to shed. The phone rang and rang, and each time it did, she felt more weight on her chest.

Please, Mom, pick up.

"*The person you are trying to reach—*"

Click.

She stuffed the phone into her sweatpants' pocket, crying into her hands. The backdoor opened, and Deryk slunk out into the misty day. He approached Mia from behind, wanting to lay a hand on her shoulder as she cried.

Mia turned around and removed her hands from her face, having heard the back door open. She faced Deryk, stopping him in his tracks. Her short hair gently billowed in the wind, like tall grass in a field. As Deryk opened his arms to give Mia a hug, she skirted around him, racing back into the house.

Deryk tried to appear as if his ego was secure despite it sitting atop a trembling pedestal at the moment. He ran after her, just catching sight of her barreling up the stairs.

"*I can't believe you!*" he heard her call.

Deryk ran up the staircase after her, fearful something horrible might happen to Mia. When he reached the doorway, Mia was bearing down on Jack, pointing in his face. Jack's face was red with tears and fear as he screamed for help.

"*You selfish bastard! How dare you ask me for a child after all this?! Who do you think you are?!*"

Jack defensively held up his hands between himself and Mia, wailing. Deryk stood in the doorway, unsure how to intervene. Should he carry Mia away and calm her down? Or would this only aggravate her and point her anger in his direction? Should he attack Jack and take Mia's side, obviously? Or would that also only point Mia's fury at him?

Mia reared her hand back and swung down, her palm catching Jack's blubbery cheek with a loud *smack!*

Deryk rushed into the room, pulling Mia into the hallway. She grunted and tried to drag herself away, to take herself back into her bedroom—her new fighting cage.

Her car sat outside, filled to the brim with boxes and a full tank, yet Mia could see herself doing nothing but beating the shit out of Jack. Anger seethed out of her as she fought Deryk off. He clambered to keep his grip on her waist when her elbow swung back and caught him in the temple. A fiery pain exploded from the impact site, knocking his grip loose. Mia fought to keep her footing, clawing for the doorframe, and made her way back into the bedroom.

Jack screamed from the bed, throwing his arms around, while Deryk struggled with his dizzy head. He made his way back to the door as Mia clenched her fist, threw it back, and nailed Jack in the cheek.

It was a glancing blow, surprising for how easily the target could have been acquired. Even someone who'd never fought before could have at least hit Jack in the nose. It wasn't a lack of aim that prevented Mia from striking him somewhere where it mattered. The last, fleeting bit of doubt ran through her mind as she propelled her fist forward, causing her to move her aim to the side of his face. Nonetheless, Jack cried out.

The creamy flesh where Mia's fist struck quickly turned strawberry red, before fading to a beet-like purple. Jack screamed like a child with a fever, his entire body jiggling with each sob. Mia neither felt better nor worse, but her knuckles hurt.

Without a word, she stormed out of the room and stomped down the stairs. She snatched up her car keys, opened the front door wide, and let herself through it, slamming it behind herself.

Deryk stood in the dank bedroom, dazed.

He watched Jack hold his face and cry for quite some time. He looked up from between his fingers and asked, "*Who are you?*"

Deryk shrugged his shoulders. "I'm your new caretaker."

Mia drove as quickly as she could to get away from her prison-like house. Burning out in the driveway, her tires screeched as she turned onto the road that would lead her from this oppressive life.

No more Jack. No more cooking. No more cleaning.

She ran through all the things she wouldn't have to do anymore in her mind as she raced through tall pines, weaving from left to right on the asphalt snake that led through the mountains she had called home for quite some time. A mix of tears and sweat cooled her skin as fresh air swept through the car's open windows. She had told herself she wouldn't cry. Every day, as she packed more and more of her possessions, she said she would not cry for Jack. She said she would not have an outburst, and there she was, speeding down a dangerous road having struck her husband multiple times.

She hoped Deryk could deal with Jack. And she hoped Jack would continue his journey through getting healthy again. She worried about him, but as she drove, she worried more for herself.

Days of driving lie ahead of her, and she was the only one she had to talk to. Emotions and thoughts freely swam through her mind. Even just driving down the road, which would eventually lead to a highway, Mia's mind ran in circles. From contemplating returning home and apologizing to Jack, to thinking back in time to nights like their wedding night, to wondering if she could have poisoned his food and peacefully watched him go.

As she sped along the road, her car being the only one beside the trees, Mia felt something moving within her gut.

A baby, her mind whispered.

No.

Mia gagged. She wrenched the wheel over, quickly pulling herself off of the road and into the gravel that preceded the forest. Throwing her door open, she heaved up bile and chunks of mango.

A horn sounded from behind her car, speeding toward her. She looked up, spit still dripping from her chin to catch sight of a truck rapidly approaching her. Having just barely gotten off the road, her door hung open into the lane.

Mia pulled herself inside and slammed the door just as the truck sped past. The driver hadn't slowed down, and she thought she could hear him screaming at her through rolled down windows.

Shaking and out of breath, she thought, *So this is the outside world.*

Chapter Six: Cheesy Penises and Bloody Assholes

"Jack, you have to eat." Deryk stood next to the bed Jack hadn't moved from in over twenty-four hours.

"*No.*"

Deryk took a deep breath, the smell of a *very* used diaper filling his nostrils. "Well, I at least need to get this diaper off of you."

Jack turned his head to look at Deryk, his eyes narrowing on him. "*You'd like that wouldn't you?*"

"What?"

Jack shook his head. "*Sick fucker.*" He thrusted his finger in Deryk's face. "*You're not seeing my dick, you pervert!*"

Deryk threw up his hands and left the room, thinking, *I can't say I blame the woman for hitting him.* He shook his head, hands on his hips, when an idea came to him.

"Hey, Jack," he said, peeking into the room, "don't you have a video to make today?"

"I don't wanna." Jack pouted.

Jesus, has he always acted like a toddler?

"Well, Jack, you don't really have a choice in the matter." Deryk ran to the bed and snatched up Jack's phone before he could move for it himself. "It's either we make a live stream with you half-naked, dirty, full diapered, in bed, *or* we get you all tidied up in your favorite shirt and get you something nice to eat for your fans." He smiled. "*Your choice.*"

Jack kept a sharp gaze on him but smiled. "You don't know my password."

Deryk made an o with his lips. "Oh, don't I?" He tried 2-0-1-1, the phone vibrating to let him know he hadn't gotten it right.

Jack chuckled. "See!"

Deryk laughed back, typing in 2-0-1-9. The phone opened, and Jack's laughter ceased. "*See,* I knew you'd care about your channel more." He opened an app and hovered his thumb over the live stream button, turning the screen so Jack could see. "So, what's it going to be?"

Jack sat in the tub, like a pile of dough in water. His face expressed all the frustration he had within him, bruised cheek and all.

Deryk stood outside the tub, wearing a vinyl smock and two mittens with scrubbing pads on them.

"What's your soap of choice?" Deryk asked.

"I don't use soap."

Deryk's face scrunched as if he'd sucked on a lemon. "You—what do you mean?"

"It irritates my skin, so Mia had to stop using it."

"Yeah, no, we're not doing that." Deryk shook his head, slipping off a glove. He dug in the duffle bag by the door and opened the door briefly to gulp in fresh air. Returning to the tub, he said, "Okay, so this is hypoallergenic, and it actually smells really nice."

Jack shook his head violently. "I *can't use* soap."

"We'll try it, okay?"

"No!"

Deryk dipped a glove into the water and scrubbed the bar of soap onto it. Jack watched the suds form, his head still shaking. When Deryk reached for Jack's arm, he slapped him away.

"*I said no!*"

"*Listen here, you shit!*" Deryk's voice had taken on the commanding tone of a drill sergeant. He leaned into Jack's face and pointed a finger close to his nose. "I deal with *all kinds* of people. Disabled. Old. Paralyzed. Morbidly obese. But *your kind* are the *worst!*"

Jack recoiled. "My kind?"

"Yes, the kind that sit on their asses all day and eat and eat and *eat!* The kind that do it to themselves and hate everyone that tries to help."

Jack lunged forward and snapped, "You know, there are people with eating disorders!"

Deryk shook his head. "Jack." His tone was even and calm. "Is it about the food or is it about the views?"

Jack's jaw set, then relaxed as his eyes fell to the water. His hands found his face as he began to sob. "*I'm trying to do better!*" he cried out.

Deryk put a hand on his shoulder. "I know, buddy, but you have to let me help. That beautiful woman left because you hurt her."

Deryk's words were met with nothing more than sobs.

"She cares about you more than *anyone* on this planet, man, and you gave her the cold shoulder even as she gave you the world."

Jack cried harder, echoing in the bathroom.

"You have to do *better.*"

Deryk scrubbed on Jack's back as the man gently cried. Layers of dead skin began clumping onto the glove, so much so that Deryk had to move over to the sink to rinse the glove off before moving to another section of Jack's monstrous back. His skin was speckled with bulbous acne, most of it ready to explode. Deryk rubbed these spots, carefully squeezing a few. When one popped, he flinched, watching the pus ooze onto the glove.

Like butter, he thought.

A rubber glove within the scrubbing mitten protected his skin, but Deryk couldn't help but feel itchy washing Jack. He drained the tub and wetted the glove with warm water and soap.

"What are you doing?" Jack asked, sniveling away the tears he'd spent the last twenty minutes crying.

Deryk handed Jack the glove. "It's going to take the both of us to get you clean."

"I just took a bath last night." Jack huffed, his skin damp and cold.

"Listen," Deryk took a deep breath, keeping Jack's feelings in mind, "Mia did her best, but you need to be *cleaned.*"

Jack looked down at himself, the view consisting of his belly laying atop his thighs and hanging over his knees. He thought of Mia asking when the last time they cleaned under his *flap* was and sighed.

"*Fine.*"

Jack took the glove and gripped his stomach with one hand. He pulled upward, but no movement was made. His arm trembled as he tried harder. Deryk stepped in, using both hands to lift the front of Jack's stomach like the hood of a car. The smell caused his grip to slip, but he kept the weight up, pretending his mistake was caused by wet skin. Jack scrubbed his crotch, grunting with effort. Deryk averted his eyes, hoping the smell would come off his clothes later that night. The crawling sensation that drove Jack to his brink at times alleviated itself under the scrubbing glove. He forced the glove into crevices and under mounds of skin, the feeling unlike any he'd experienced in a long time. Carefully, he wiped around his penis, unsure how his body would react to the sought-after contact. His body shuddered.

"*Alright, let's rinse you off,*" Deryk said, removing one of his hands from the flap to grab the shower head. He turned the water on, letting it warm.

Jack removed the glove from underneath his stomach. Instead of the bright blue it once was, the glove hung, defeated, in Jack's hand, the color of dark pus. Balls of dead skin, which seemed to squirm, filled its scrubby material and the smell of sour cheese emanated from it.

Deryk kept himself from gagging. Fifteen years of working as an in-home care nurse—fifteen years of wiping shit from his face and washing other people's piss out of his clothes—and nothing had ever disgusted him as much as this man's cheese.

"Just, uh, set it in the tub. I'll rinse it out."

Jack threw the glove into the bottom of the tub where it splattered in dirty water. Deryk sprayed it off but ultimately knew it would end up in the trash.

"Alright, let's rinse." He assisted Jack in lifting his gut again and gently washed it out. Chunks of yellow, brown, and black skin fell out between his legs, sticking to the sides of the tub. Deryk tried to keep the cringe from showing on his face, but not much could be done.

Jack shook his head, thinking about how right Mia was. He looked at Deryk in awe, astounded this man was okay washing another man's body, especially his.

Deryk set down Jack's gut, imagining the amount of chafing that was to follow.

I gotta get this man some good lotion to keep his dick from rubbing off, he thought.

When he was handed the shower head, Jack moved it around, allowing the water over his entire body. Deryk retrieved another scrubbing glove from his bag and gave it to Jack, who took it with a smile. He scoured his arms and the top of his belly but struggled to reach his shoulders and the back of his neck. Deryk offered to do so for him and gave him a bottle of soap for his face.

"It's gentler."

Jack poured out too much soap and rubbed it on his face, top of his head, and neck. When he looked at Deryk, the nurse couldn't help but laugh.

"Now that's a clean man," he said, giving Jack the shower head again.

It had taken almost two hours, but Jack felt cleaner and in a better mindset, almost as if he'd lost fifty pounds.

As Deryk dried him off, he asked, "How much weight do you think I lost washing up like that?"

Deryk shook his head. "Let's try not to think of that." He gave Jack a towel to dry off with and thought about the man's ass. "Hey." He paused. "When was the last time you scrubbed your butt?"

Jack shook his head. "I don't know. Mia usually uses wipes when she takes off my diaper."

Deryk sighed. "You're going to have to stand." Jack's eyes widened. "*Stand?*"

"Yeah." He nodded, reaching for Jack's hands.

"No, I, I don't think I can, especially in the tub." The throbbing in his ribs thumped faster with his heart rate.

"Jack, you can do it." Deryk smiled, looking into Jack's eyes. "I'll help you."

He nodded, looking down at the sides of the tub.

"You'll have to face the wall, so I can, you know, wash your butt."

Jack nodded, grabbing the handle on the wall for support and pulling. Grunting, his skin began to tear from the surface of the tub's built-in seat. Deryk grabbed under his arms and lifted. He was a lean man but used to this sort of work.

Jack felt the force of his weight sink to his feet as he wobbled onto unsteady legs, mainly keeping his weight on the one not cast.

Deryk gasped.

Purple and red laced skin lined a section of brown flesh on Jack's butt crack. Standing caused pieces to roll off and sections to break open and bleed.

"Jack?"

"Yeah?"

"Your butt feel okay?"

"Oh, I haven't felt much of my butt in months."

Deryk nodded. "Oh, okay."

He debated whether he should rush Jack to the hospital or leave the skin alone. He feared it would only irritate it if he washed it, but also didn't want Jack to die of an infection that he could have easily healed.

Deryk chose the middle option, opting to keep Jack home but also clean his butt. He sprayed water onto the sore, expecting Jack to suddenly flinch. When he didn't, Deryk sighed.

Caked on feces plopped into the bathtub, and brown water ran off the clumps. Skin followed along, washed down with blood and scabs. Deryk took his scrubby glove and cautiously pulled at indiscernible pieces, worried they might still be attached.

Jack struggled to stay on his feet but felt a sense of pride in his chest. He hadn't stood in at least two months. Every muscle in his legs strained, his ribs throbbed, and his heart felt as if it were about to explode, but he was *standing*.

Deryk softly scraped at the rough skin, watching the brown wash away and leave behind a sickly, bruised purple that seeped with fresh blood. He was confident it wasn't infected yet as no pus presented itself beneath the layer of dead skin and shit, but he still felt the need for a topical antibiotic.

"You good?" he asked, stepping away from the tub.

Jack nodded and said, "*Yes,*" enthusiastically.

Deryk rushed over to his bag, digging around for the tube of cream as quickly as possible with his one clean hand.

Jack held on tight to the handles, swaying a bit. He could feel the slick surface of the tub on the underside of his feet and imagined himself slipping and falling.

Would it crack my head open?

Deryk looked at Jack, seeing the large man's arms tremble as they clutched the handles that he was surprised held to the wall. The tub creaked, and Deryk also imagined Jack slipping and falling. He could see his bald head smack the relentless tile wall and slide down it. The image that came to mind was that of a cracked egg. The yolk and white membrane would slip free of Jack's shattered skull, draining across the floor of the tub.

His fingers found the ointment, and he rushed back over to help support Jack. "It's almost over," he said, globbing the cream onto the glove. He smeared it around, hoping it would fix the problem.

The door to the bathtub opened, and Deryk handed Jack a towel. He was able to quickly wrap it about his waist while standing and take one step toward his chair before his hand shot out to grab a handle.

Deryk's eyes widened, and he snatched up Jack's arms, helping to stabilize him. "One thing at a time, dude." He chuckled and so did Jack as he fell into his chair.

A mug of hot chocolate sat on Jack's bedside table. The TV was on, playing an old cartoon, and Deryk cleaned the kitchen counter downstairs. Jack sat up in bed, feeling alright for himself, despite his situation. He could hear Deryk whistling in the kitchen.

Jack had hope. Just a little bit of it, but it was there.

Mia would come home. Deryk could leave, but they would remain friends. Rochelle would love him but from afar, and Mia would get pregnant with his baby boy after he lost some weight. He would open the channel to Mia and their son, making it about family matters and DIYs.

Fun recipes for kids and how they can help, he thought. *Homemade dinners for babies* and *Where to take your baby on their first road trip*.

Jack smiled.

The number of views would skyrocket.

Mukbang was on its way out, and Jack knew it. He'd been scrolling his feed for weeks, only to be bombarded with baby videos. No matter the platform or account he used, babies filled his screen.

Pandemic babies are built different!

I can't wait to see what this little bump is! Vote on my story whether you think it's a boy or a girl!

My baby loves *this stuff! Be sure to check out the link in my bio!*

It was perfect. People have babies every day, and most of them are inexperienced parents looking to someone on their phone to guide them through raising a child.

And I'm going to be that person.

Jack hit his plateau of followers approximately two months prior. He knew it when his videos became stagnant, and the same people were viewing them. They commented the same things on every video: *Awesome!* or *a string of emojis no one understands* or *That looks yummy!*

Jack could strangle each and every one of them; snap their neck like a popsicle stick because, quite frankly, he hated the person he'd become.

He hated eating so much. He hated losing his body to something so superficial. He hated pushing Mia away but felt nothing but anger in his chest. And worst of all, he hated living in a chair for these fools. Ever since he broke his leg, he'd been confined to the chair.

I can't believe you didn't post the video of you falling to your channel. It would have hit the million-view mark for sure.

Everyone would have laughed at you, but it would have grown your following.

"Jack?" Deryk asked from the doorway.

Jack had begun to cry. Little droplets streamed down his cheeks. His face was red, even in the dim light from the TV. He quickly swept them away, thankful Deryk was present. He smiled.

"Yeah?"

"I'm headed home for the night, but this," he walked into the room and set a pager on the nightstand, "is my pager. Just press this button if you need help."

Just as soon as they'd left, Jack's tears returned. "You're leaving?"

Deryk's eyes widened as he realized what this meant for Jack. "Yeah, buddy. My two-year-old is going to be put to bed in about an hour, and I'd like to see her."

"You have a baby?"

Deryk nodded. "Yeah, and she likes to cuddle with her daddy."

Jack looked at the floor and nodded. "I'll see you tomorrow, Deryk."

"You sure will. I'll lock the door on my way out."

"Okay."

Jack hadn't been alone at night in a very long time. The last time he'd slept in an empty house was close to fifteen years ago, if not longer. He had roommates in college and Mia to cuddle with after he'd gotten his degree.

A degree in graphic design collected dust on the wall in his office downstairs. It initially helped when he and Mia began making their videos, but now they had someone to do all their promos and art and editing. All Jack had to do was press *record* and act like the fat fool he was.

He shook his head. All of these people who saw him every day—they spoke to him via comments and likes and DMs—yet he felt like no one saw him.

Eating was fun in the beginning. It was like a challenge. Then the weight added on, and he began to feel sluggish and tired all the time. Then more weight, but with that weight came followers and money.

Jack thought of how it all started: the one video in Bologna, Italy. They'd recorded *hours* of material as *The Travelers* in shops. Tired of narrating their lives to a small digital camera, they'd agreed to keep it off for dinner, but Jack couldn't resist. Mia's hair had been perfectly messy, and her dark eyes glowed orange from the candle on the table. The restaurant's lighting was peacefully dull inside, and the charcoal brick walls absorbed the light from the candles. It was *her* and only *her* present in front of him. Her ivory skin glowed with youth, and his hands begged to touch her bare shoulders. He'd pulled out the camera, recording her as she sipped on wine. She'd laughed, asking why he broke their promise.

"*I couldn't resist,*" he'd said.

"*Ah.*" She nodded and gave him model poses.

Jack shook his head in awe, wondering how she'd never made it to larger runways.

You. That's why, a small voice said, interrupting his memory. Jack hushed the voice.

Mia had convinced him to hand her the camera, and just as he did, a waiter appeared from the shadows and brought them their food. He'd gotten spaghetti and meatballs, something Mia shook her head at.

"*We're in Italy and you get something I could make at home* any time."

"*Well, you gotta try the classics,*" he'd said, forking a meatball.

Mia recorded him eating, asking questions between his bites.

"*What do you think they seasoned the meatballs with?*"

He shrugged his shoulders, chewing.

"*Well, what does it taste like?*"

"*Basil. Lots of basil.*" He wiped his tongue on the roof of his mouth, wondering who had cooked his food. Twirling his fork in noodles doused in red sauce, he took a bite.

Mia giggled from behind the camera. "*What's got you making that face?*"

Jack chewed. "*More basil,*" he said after swallowing.

He'd finished his plate on camera, critiquing the meal along the way.

"*I feel like this meal was prepared by an American living here in Italy.*"

Mia laughed so hard the camera shook.

Later that night, Jack edited the video, and he posted it the following day. Two-hundred thousand views had appeared in the first hour, breaking a million by the end of the day. He and Mia were *astonished*.

"*It had to be because you were eating,*" Mia said.

"*Oh my God.*"

A year later, Covid struck the world, halting all travel. *The Travelers* were now doing nothing but *traveling* from their couch to the kitchen.

"*Jack, what are we going to do?*"

More people than *ever* started channels.

"*We could cook and share recipes,*" Jack offered.

"*There's a ton of accounts doing that, Jack. We're already on a down streak, I don't see how we can come back from this.*"

Jack scoured their content, looking for anything people liked. Mia studied other channels, looking for anything they could do better.

That's when she realized they were nothing but a couple who shopped in parts of the world others couldn't get to. People lived vicariously through them, and that's all they were worth to people. They had no talents or insight into the world.

"*Jack, I think it's time we thought about something else.*"

"*No.*" He'd been frustrated, having gone through hours of their content, hundreds of comments, and notebooks full of ideas he'd had over the last eight years.

"*Jack, you could set some of these people down into a room empty of everything but their camera, and they could make a* show. *They could entertain an audience for hours with just their voice and facial expressions, but we* are not *those people.*" It hurt her to say so, but she knew deep within herself, she could do nothing but be pretty and go to pretty places.

"*No!*" Jack snapped, getting up from his desk quickly. Mia stared into his eyes, the dark circles around them drawing her in. "*No. Mia, we're entertaining in so many other ways. I just know we can figure out something.*"

Their *exclusive* channel had only lasted a month.

"*We have chemistry on camera, Mia. I know we can make this work.*" Jack constructed their page, figured out their brand, and decided what content to share. He began studying angles for boudoir photography.

"*Jack, I don't know that I'm comfortable with this.*"

"*Mia, you were a model before we got together. There's nothing to worry about.*"

Photos of Mia hidden behind nothing but a sheet or a book began flooding their page, and slowly but surely, the coverings got smaller and smaller. Three weeks into it, Mia decided to take control.

"*I am not going to be the only one on camera here. We might as well call it* Mia's Whore Photos *at this point!*"

"*They're boudoir photos, Mia. There's nothing whorish about them.*"

"*Yeah, well the guys jacking off to them would have something else to say about that.*" She slumped onto the couch, the one covered in chip crumbs and soda stains. Cleaning hadn't been on either of their minds.

"*Jack, we were supposed to do this together.*"

She looked up at him with sad eyes, and it broke him. "*Fine. Get the camera.*"

Jack hadn't been to the gym in weeks, and his diet had shifted from fresh food to frozen and delivered meals as going out to shop was frowned upon. He simply wasn't as toned as he used to be.

Mia posed him, naked, in front of the fireplace, where he held just a log in front of himself.

"*Hey, why does my first photo have to be revealing?*" he asked, a smirk on his face.

Mia did not return the sentiment, answering curtly, "*Because I've been almost nude in sixty photos that you've posted, and you haven't posted a single one of yourself.*"

She snapped the photo, and it went live later that night. Jack's smirk had been broken, leaving him with a smoldering look of disapproval aimed at the camera lens.

Out of 992 subscribers, only sixteen were women.

Only five subscribers remained by the next day.

"*What happened?!*" Jack asked.

Mia had shaken her head, pinching between her eyes. "*You built an audience of horny people attracted to naked* women*, Jack.*"

And so came the downfall of their exclusive page and every other platform they hosted on.

"*What can we do?!*" he asked.

And once again, Jack went through all his notes, all their videos, and all their comments. A week of him stuffed in his study with nothing more than glasses of water passed, when it hit him. He finally decided to have a full meal, and Mia warmed up some udon noodles in the microwave. Jack ate them in front of his computer when it went into sleep mode, revealing his haggard reflection. Dark circles rung his eyes. His skin had broken out with cystic acne, a combination of stress, diet, and lack of showering.

But the noodles in his mouth reminded him of a video.

He'd been focused on the wrong part of the video. It wasn't his supple wife's look of innocence that had gotten them followers.

No.

It had been him in the same position as he was in that moment: stuffing his face with noodles.

Mukbang.

That was it! That was the million-dollar idea that he could do from his house.

"*Mia! Mia!*" he shouted.

He found her in the kitchen and grabbed her shoulders, shaking her.

"Mukbang! *Mukbang!*"

Sitting up in his bed three years later, he wondered where his life would be if Mia had continued her boudoir career. Meanwhile, Mia sat in her car in a gas station parking lot wondering the same thing.

She also wondered what her life would be like had she never met Jack. She'd most likely be a model on the biggest runways just as she'd dreamed. Walking next to the biggest names in fashion, wearing the best brands. Instead, she traveled the world with a man obsessed with followers.

There has to be an angle for his change of heart. A baby? Something is wrong.

The gas station sat halfway into Nevada, and she thought about their possible child while staring at the front of the convenience store. A half-eaten pastry lay on her dashboard, strawberry filling oozing from the center. The taste was thick in her mouth, gumming up her tongue.

The bright white lights above her car were giving her a migraine, and she wished the pump wouldn't pump so leisurely. With her window cracked, she could hear it ticking slowly, about as sluggish as the filling oozed from her pastry.

Bam!

There was a man at her window. Mia looked into his eyes, stunned by their brightness. For a moment she thought of Deryk, but this man was clearly stricken with addiction. Her hand reached for the door lock just as the man yanked on the handle. She screamed, snatching the door and slamming it shut. Smacking the door lock, her heart beat fast.

The man laughed from the other side of the thin glass. "What's the matter, doll? Don't wanna play?"

She thought of the gun she'd packed away and left in the trunk. Panting, she had no words for this man. She narrowed her eyes at him and set her jaw, hoping to feign strength when she felt as if she were teetering off of a cliff.

"Guess the pretty girl doesn't want any money," he said, chuckling.

The gas pump sounded a final, loud *click,* announcing it was finished pumping out the thirty dollars she put in. The man jumped at the noise and skirted away from her car.

Mia sat, the only sounds being the music from the gas pumps around her and the thumping of her heart.

Rochelle listened to the rapid drumming of her own heart, thunderous in her ears. She'd enjoyed the sex, if not only for a moment, but by the time it was all said and done, she found herself repulsed. Johnson lay next to her, his eyes closed and facing away from her.

She felt trapped in the monotony of it all. Her job was nothing but a dead end. Her boss was nothing but a pervert. And she could never have the life she wanted for herself.

Carefully, she got up to go to the bathroom. Johnson's house was awfully free of personal belongings—or even fixtures—and Rochelle had a hunch she was sleeping with a man squatting in an abandoned apartment.

Rochelle peed, wiped herself up, and all the while she thought:

Twenty-seven. Living in an apartment that reeks of weed and BO from the guys that come around. Working at a greeting card company that sucks and barely affording rent.

Sleeping with my boss sounded sexy at first, but—

She farted into the toilet by accident, hoping to have not woken Johnson. Wide-eyed, she covered her butthole with a clump of toilet paper to deaden the sound as another slipped free.

—he's no connoisseur of the bedroom. And if my pantry wasn't empty—hmmph—I wouldn't even be here.

She got up, not flushing, and washed her hands quietly. Her reflection stared back at her from a water spotted mirror. Two handprints sat inches from either side of the reflection of her face. Curious, she set her hands into these prints, realizing with a bit more revulsion what they implied.

I guess this slob gets tail.

She scanned over herself, completely naked in the drafty bathroom, standing on grit-covered tile that reeked of old bleach and piss. Her ponytail had been wrecked by Johnson's unsteady grip. Rochelle tore the hair tie free and looked around for a brush, only to be let down. She combed her fingers through the ratty mess in an attempt to pull it back up.

Man couldn't pull hair right if a gun was put to his head.

With a new ponytail and a newfound loss of respect for herself, Rochelle headed back to the bedroom. A streetlamp dimly illuminated the room, shining on Johnson's mattress which sat directly on the floor with no sheets to hug it. Only a few throw blankets kept their skin from what only God knew was on those sheets.

She shuddered as Johnson ripped a fat snore and decided it was her time to head out.

With her clothes on and bag in hand, Rochelle made her way to the front door. When she saw it, she couldn't believe she allowed herself to be vulnerable.

A lock, like one you'd see on a shed, wrapped itself around a piece of metal on the doorframe. This piece of metal had been inserted into another piece of metal screwed into the front door.

Fuck.

She spun around, looking at the backdoor.

Nothing but plywood.

Something stirred in the front entryway, and Rochelle rushed to the back of the house.

Gotta be an open window.

She turned the corner in front of Johnson's bedroom, meeting his gaze.

"Hello, Rochelle," he said, sitting on the corner of the bed, naked. His knees were bent as his butt slowly depressed the corner of the mattress, making him look like a middle-aged bullfrog. "Did you think that fart wouldn't wake me?" He laughed. "That fart probably woke the *neighbors*."

Rochelle gasped.

"Surprised to see me in my own apartment?" He stood up with no effort or loss of balance.

"This isn't even your apartment, Johnson." She shook her head, wishing she hadn't shown up for the date.

"*It is if they can't get the locks off.*" He chuckled, making Rochelle's skin crawl. "For a short time at least."

"Well, I'd like to leave now, Mr. David."

"You know, that's not even my real name."

Rochelle was appalled. She'd always questioned the name, but she supposed she'd never questioned the person behind the name. "Well, what's your real name?"

"Oh, if I told you that, I'd have to *kill you*." He took a step toward her. "But I was already thinking of that anyway."

"Why?" Rochelle's inner monologue laughed at her question, such an odd thing to ask in such a time.

Johnson, or whatever his name was, scoffed. "Why?" He threw his arms up, the loose skin on his biceps jiggling. "Look at this place. Do you think a sane person stays in a place like this?"

She looked around, a burning feeling building in her gut. "No, I guess not."

"*Exactly!* I'm bonkers, and I'd just love to let out some of that frustration on *you*."

Rochelle laughed, causing his eyes to widen. "You think *you're crazy?*"

"Well, yeah."

"I just showed up to an abandoned apartment with my boss, who's at least twice my age, and *fucked him* on a dirty mattress on the floor."

"Well, your apartment isn't much cleaner."

Rochelle was about to say something before she stopped. "*How do you know that?*"

"Well, I've been inside of it before."

He'd said it so matter-of-factly, like it was just common sense to be within her home, within the place she slept and had her dreams.

"*That's it.*" She threw down her bag and rushed Johnson, swinging her fist and connecting. His jaw was sent sideways, a tooth flitting away to smack the wall with a few droplets of blood. Three inches taller, fifty-two pounds heavier, Rochelle had the upper hand.

His naked body flailed, falling into a crumpled pile on the floor, ass up. Rochelle lifted her foot and stamped down her heel. Unexpectedly, it punctured what she thought was his buttcheek in the darkness.

When he cried out, "*My asshole!*" Rochelle didn't know what to think.

She pulled her foot back, the heel staying buried in Johnson's rectum. He was crying and screaming, louder than any fart of hers could be, and when he tried to stand, he fell back to his knees, whimpering.

Rochelle looked around as he hollered at her.

"*Take it out of my ass! For the love of* God! *Please take it out of my ass!*"

Downstairs, a young man looked up at his ceiling in utter confusion.

A carpenter's hammer glittered in the streetlamp's light. Johnson heard the head of it scrape against the floor before turning around.

"*What's your real name?*" she asked through gritted teeth.

His eyes met hers, and he whispered, "David Johnson."

With a strength Rochelle didn't realize she had, she bore down on Johnson's face with the hammer, shattering his cheekbone in one swing.

He cried out, mewling like an injured animal, and flopped to the floor. On his side he lay, twitching and clawing at his face.

Johnson bled on the floor in twin streams from the crack in his skull.

Rochelle kicked off her remaining heel and raised the hammer again. She swung downward, striking the back of his head with a wet *thwap*, and Johnson splayed limp with a hammer in his brain.

Rochelle stood over him, heavily breathing for a good five minutes before coming to. Surely the police would be on their way soon if there were *neighbors* in this area.

She ran out of the bedroom, scooping up her bag, and dashing into the living area. A big chunk of concrete sat on the floor in the corner. She picked this up, aimed it at the window beside where a TV would go, and chucked it. It impacted, shattering the glass before falling three floors along with the remains of the window.

Using her bag, she broke the glass away from the frame. Looking over the sill, she saw the drop was into an alleyway, but the balcony was only a few feet over, around a corner. Slinging her bag over her shoulder, she hopped onto the window's edge and threw her legs over. Catching a footing on a small ledge with her right foot, she was able to swing her left foot and hook it onto the balcony. She took a deep breath, bracing to shift her weight, and went for it. Her left hand caught the railing as her right foot landed, and there she hung, successful in the first part of her mission.

Over the railing, she stood on the balcony overlooking a small suburban slum, and next to the balcony was a fire escape.

Oh, thank God.

On her way down the stairs, she could think of nothing in her apartment that she wanted to keep. In fact, she could think of nothing in the whole town she wanted to keep besides her car. She had nothing left.

It was parked at the curb across the street from David's apartment building, and as she approached, she only had one place in mind.

Ding!

Jack rubbed his eyes, having been staring at the ceiling for the past two hours.

Do you ever take visitors?

Jack's heart thudded in his chest.

Depends…

Depends on what?

Who it is

It's me. Duh.

You really coming up here?

I wouldn't ask if I wasn't.

…

Send your addy, Daddy.

Rochelle set the GPS on her phone to Jack's address as she drove north on the freeway. Cool air blew in, drying the sweat and blood on her body.

From a young age, Rochelle knew she was different. Her father liked to tell her so with the back of his hand. Her mother liked to tell her so with utter silence. Rochelle vividly remembered the day she got her license and never saw her parents again. She drove down the freeway, windows down, to an unfamiliar place, much as she was doing again. Driving was, and always would be, her escape. In a country with 3.8 million square miles, there was always a distance to wedge between her and her problems.

Jack sat in his bed in anticipation.

Rochelle. Here?

The thought made his body tingle into his toes and through the top of his head, even with memories of Mia dancing around in his mind. He felt a squirming presence in his groin as he peered at Rochelle's page. She was plump and curvaceous in all the places Mia wasn't, and he couldn't wait to get a handful.

Although Mia's absence was heavy on his chest, some of the weight was removed with the thought of Rochelle's appearance.

Jack looked down at himself. Over his CPAP mask, he could see the bulge under the blanket that was his gut. He imagined having to pick it up and out of the way so Rochelle could sit on his lap. Embarrassment burned thickly in his head.

What have I done to myself?

Mia drove east, her windows rolled up tight and heater on full blast; the hot air from the vents dried her tears.

She'd called her mother at least ten times on the road, all with no answer. The lines on the asphalt blurred through tears, her chest shattered into a million jagged pieces.

What if something's happened to them?

Mia thought of the possibility of showing up at her childhood home in North Carolina and finding her parents dead on the floor or in their bed. She thought of how they could have died.

Frozen in place from a heart attack or peacefully asleep from COVID or hanging from a noose.

Maybe they decided to try out an art project and splatter the walls with their brains, Mia.

She shook her head, hands clenched on the steering wheel.

Yeah, they loaded up that little revolver they used to keep under the cash register, and—BOOM—shot themselves. Little fragments of bone and chunks of brain matter all over the living room wall and all those photos of you.

"*SHUT UP!*" Mia screamed.

She'd driven for a while and made it three-quarters of the way through Nevada. There was a truck stop up ahead, its fluorescent aura glowing. Had she not had to pee, Mia would have flown by without a thought.

It was dark, cold, and she was alone.

The station was daunting with its rows of semi-trucks and bustling, zombie-esque patrons circling the pumps and store. Mia had a pocketknife with her, but she wondered if it would be enough. She parked at a pump and got out. The driver in front of her, a young man in his early twenties with bags under his eyes large enough to be considered carry-ons, nodded at her. She gave a small smile in return and hurried to the front door of the store.

Cigarette smoke plumed in her face as she opened the glass door. A man standing at a circular counter in the middle of the store gave her a small wave as she walked in. It was warm, allowing her to relax a bit and remove her hands from her pockets.

Rows of snacks and candy met her as she glided through. The air in the bathroom was almost freezing, making Mia tense up again. She peed, shivering, and washed up in the sink without a glance at herself. Shaking her head as she left the bathroom, she wondered how she was going to stay awake long enough to drive further. There was no room in her back-seat to rest and barely enough to lean her driver's seat back.

Turning a corner, she was met with a pair of slot machines—pristine and shiny, as if they'd just been dropped off. The leather chair in front of it looked surprisingly comfortable, and Mia quickly found herself in it.

She located a twenty out of her wallet, which was fat with bills after a trip to the bank. The slot machine greedily sucked it in, chiming with satisfaction. Mia grabbed the knob at the side of the machine, her eyes glittering from the neon lights, and yanked down. The slots rolled.

Jewel. Cherry. Seven.

Three Sevens. Diamond. Bar.

Around and around it went, finally landing in order from left to right.

Jewel. Jewel. Jewel.

"*No way!*" Mia raised her arms in victory, having won fifty credits. Being a twenty-five-cent machine, that got her twelve dollars and fifty cents.

She slammed down the knob again, catching the attention of everyone in the sleepy convenience store.

Jewel. Diamond. Cherry.

"*Damn it,*" Mia cursed under her breath. She'd bet nine lines, a total of two dollars and twenty-five cents.

She lowered her bet to twenty-five cents, and each time she pressed the button, it chimed.

"*Please be something good,*" she whispered under her breath. This time, she tapped the button instead of slamming the crank.

They did not fall into the first line, rather, diagonally, three diamonds fell into place.

"*Damn it!*" If Mia had bet five, she would have won three hundred credits. "*Shit!*" she hissed.

She increased her bet to five credits and smacked the button.

Diamond. Diamond.

The entire slot machine began to light up, glowing red. The final slot rolled and rolled.

Jewel. Cherry. Seven. Three Sevens. Diamond. Three. Seven. Jewel.

The diamond slid by.

"*Come on.*"

The slot slowed, resting on a jewel.

Thirty credits appeared on the screen next to her current credits, and she sighed. Mia smacked the button again, surprised the machine lit up green.

Free Spins!

"Oh my goodness," she whispered.

The machine spun itself, racking up credits with five free games. Mia held her hands together in front of her chest, watching the machine in awe. The sleepiness she felt before was gone, entirely replaced by fascination and excitement.

The machine roared with the sound of jingling coins, tallying up one-hundred credits total. Mia did the math, figuring that was twenty-five dollars. Her eyes moved up the machine, looking at the screen which displayed the numerous ways to win.

I can do better.

She tapped the *Bet Three* button and pulled down on the crank, watching the slots turn in anticipation.

Nothing.

She bet five.

Nothing.

Seven credits.

Nothing.

Nine credits.

Not even a jewel.

One credit.

Nada.

One credit.

Close! Almost. Almost.

Nine credits.

Nothing.

Nine credits.

Nothing.

Soon she was back down to the original twenty she had inserted.

I could just take it out like nothing happened.

Or you could win it all.

The digital numbers at the top of the machine said the jackpot was $13,051.

You could totally win that.

Mia felt life had cheated her. She felt she had the perfect life until COVID hit—until her husband decided to do anything for views, including destroying himself. She was owed this. The universe owed her something.

Shortly after a few games, she was given nothing but a wallet short of twenty dollars. Mia shook her head. An inkling of reassurance was there in her mind.

If you just put in twenty more dollars, you could get that jackpot.

So, at one in the morning at a truck stop in the middle of the desert, Mia slid another twenty into the slot machine.

The cashier watched from his spot at the register, shaking his head.

She ran through it quickly, betting nine almost the entire time.

"*Shit.*"

A fifty found its way from her wallet, ready to slide into the machine.

I'm this close.

And like that it was gone. Thirty minutes went by where she spent ten to get back twenty, then she lost it all again.

Tears filled her eyes.

Just one good hit.

Please.

For a moment Mia sat before the sparkling machine and thought of the lives behind and ahead of her. Behind her was an abusive man with an obsession that took precedence over her, and ahead of her was a life with her parents in the town she grew up in as a divorcee.

She slid in another fifty.

The cashier watched Mia cry and lose her cash, wondering if he should go over and stop her. She cheered quietly when she won ten bucks, and he considered what she was going through, landing on divorce. He turned his back and continued reading his magazine as people sleepily filed around the store.

Three times she had been one place away from the grand jackpot. She pushed through after winning back the money she had spent, scanning the slot for the jackpot after every bet, and after every loss, more tears rolled from her eyes. Five dollars here and fifty cents there wasn't enough. She believed thirteen thousand would heal part of her broken heart. That it would make life easier from here on out. She wouldn't have Jack's income to rely on anymore, and her parents needed her to pay part of their bills as working at chain stores didn't pay what their restaurant used to.

As her credits ran down, she began to sob, the high of her small wins diminished. Hitting zero, she covered her face in her hands, ashamed. The exhaustion returned, piling weight onto her body. Her ring bumped her nose, and Mia opened her eyes. She looked at the stone, small but decent, and ripped it off her finger. She contemplated leaving it on the slot machine for the next player before stuffing it into her pocket and crying into her hands again.

"What's got ya down, little lady?"

Mia looked up, smearing tears from her face and sniveling. A man in a large cowboy hat sat down at the slot next to her, kicking up his cowboy boot on a low ledge of the machine. In a flannel and jeans, she thought he looked like the typical cowboy.

His brown handlebar mustache really put the image together in her mind.

She crossed her arms defensively, and said, "Husband issues." The words came out sadder than she wanted them to. She wanted to sound fierce and mean, especially in a place like this.

The man smiled, his eyes soft. He appeared fully awake, as if the sun wasn't still hours away from cresting the horizon. Something about him was inviting to Mia, like she could get on the back of a horse with him and ride off into the sunset.

He shook his head with that smile still on his face. "Ah, we all been there."

Mia smiled back, sniveling again, and asked, "Yeah?"

The man seemed to lean in slightly—just enough for Mia to notice. But she did not recoil.

"Yeah." His face slackened, falling into sorrow masked by the need to remain stoic. "My wife had cancer."

Mia gasped.

"She passed away three years ago."

She reached out her hand, setting it on his forearm gently. Looking deep into his eyes, she whispered, *"I'm so sorry."*

He gave her a light smile. "It's alright."

Mia's eyebrows lifted, thinking back to the love she used to hold for Jack. "I couldn't imagine."

He waved it off with his free hand. "It's okay. We was fighting when she died."

"Oh my goodness."

"It's okay. She hit me, so I gave her too many of her pills mixed in her afternoon soup."

Mia's eyes widened, and she slowly retracted her hand. The man's smile was as welcoming as a white van's open door. What she'd mistaken for alertness so early in the morning became a deranged hardness in his eyes, something unmistakably psychotic.

He stood up quickly, causing Mia to flinch.

"Well, it was nice meeting you."

And he left.

Mia sat, shaking. She looked around, seeing that none of the other patrons had noticed her or the strange man, and the cashier had his back to her. The money she'd lost now forgotten, Mia decided to wash her face in the bathroom.

Her reflection had slipped past her earlier in the night, but upon returning, it caught her off guard. Her short hair threw itself up in clumps here and there, appearing as if it had just been butchered. The skin of her face was ashen white—no rose to her cheeks, but the bags under her eyes were a deeply bruised purple. Her bottom lip was cracked from chewing it on the drive, and her wet eyes and nose made her look like she had a cold. Vessels in her eyes had burst from crying and straining them, giving her sclera a pink glow. She wanted to scream.

Rochelle washed her hands in a gas station bathroom miles away from Mia. It had been her first stop since David's house, and she hadn't the slightest clue that she'd been driving around half covered in scumbag blood. Taking rough, brown paper towels, she soaked them in water and soap and scrubbed, rubbing her skin raw before ridding herself of the red stains.

Her jeans and T-shirt were splattered, the blood having sprayed across her sideways. Her hair was matted and messy, and her underwear were soaked in sweat and cum. She'd do anything for a shower.

Bang. Bang.

Rochelle glared at the door. "*In use, motherfucker!*"

"*Hurry up!*" someone screamed from outside.

She scoffed, shaking her head. Ripping open the door, she presented her bloody self to a cowering man outside, his face thin with drug abuse.

His eyes widened. "*Are you okay?*"

She laughed, pushing past him. "Yeah, but you should see the other guy."

He gasped, scurrying into the bathroom and slamming the door behind himself.

In her car, Rochelle brought up Jack's page. She clicked their chat and hovered over the *call* button. Rolling out of the parking lot, she tapped it.

Jack sat up in bed, his phone ringing. Deep in his sleepy mind, he hoped it would be Mia. He hoped she would say she was on her way back, that she would be through the door any minute and they could cuddle together in bed. He was sure he'd lost a few pounds, so maybe she could finally sleep in their bed with him.

It wasn't until his mind fully woke up that he realized that wasn't her ringtone and looking at the picture that appeared with the call, he saw it was Rochelle. He smiled, still unsure how to feel.

She'll make me feel better. She always does.

"Hello?"

"Hey, it's Rochelle," she said, merging onto the freeway.

"Hey, Rochelle. It's so nice to hear your voice."

She laughed. "Yeah, okay, weirdo." She paused, waiting for him to say something. When he didn't, she asked, "Why are you still up?"

"Oh, I couldn't sleep."

"What's the matter?"

A small pause followed, then Jack croaked, "Mia left."

Rochelle smirked. *No way.* "What happened?" she feigned pity.

"She just left me—just this morning."

"Aw, poor thing. I was actually looking forward to meeting her." She covered her mouth, stifling a laugh.

"Really?"

"Well, yeah, you two are iconic."

"Yeah," he took a deep breath, *"we were, weren't we?"* He sobbed.

Rochelle rolled her eyes, letting him get it out of his system before speaking. "You okay?"

"Not really." He sounded like a pouting child.

"Fucker!" Rochelle screamed.

"What?"

"Oh, sorry, someone cut me off." She flashed her lights at the car in front of her and flipped them off, despite knowing they couldn't see her in the dark.

"You still driving?"

"Yeah, but I'll be there soon. You been lonely?"

"Yeah, ever since Deryk left."

"Who's Deryk?"

"Mia hired a nurse before she left. He's been so kind to me, and he really showed me how poorly Mia was taking care of me."

"Oh, yeah?"

"Yeah, he's been so encouraging and nice. He even told me a bit about his personal life."

"Sounds like you wanna suck his dick."

Jack's face dropped, his mouth opening in a small O. "What—what do you mean?"

"Well, you just met the guy. Taking care of people is his job, Jack."

Jack mulled it over in silence, figuring she was right, but holding onto the belief Deryk was a genuinely nice guy. "I don't know, Ro—"

"I'm telling you, Jack. It's just his job."

"But he really cares."

"*I care.*"

"I know." Jack suddenly felt uncomfortable, like he was being scolded by his mother. "I'm glad you'll be here soon."

Rochelle smiled.

"What's got you coming up this way, anyway?" he asked.

"*You.*"

Jack's eyes widened. "Really? Just me?"

"Yeah." Rochelle's fingers idly picked at the rough blood stains on her jeans. "Yeah, I finished up some business here in SoCal, and now I don't have much else to look forward to. I was sort of hoping to find a place up there to live." She trailed off, leaving Jack with his thoughts.

"Well," Jack said.

She perked up.

"I have some extra space since Mia moved out. I'm pretty sure she took everything she could fit into her little car."

Rochelle beamed. "Oh, Jack, I couldn't do that to you on such short notice. I mean, I don't even have any clothes or—"

"No worries, my channel pays for *everything*."

She sighed, a fat smile on her lips. "Okay, if you insist." A bright neon motel sign lit up the sky just off of the freeway. Rochelle turned on her blinker and made her way onto the exit. "Well, Jack, I better get off. I should get some sleep before heading any further north."

Chapter Seven: Trimming the Fat

"And lift. And lift. Aaaannd *lift!*"

Jack's skin had lost some of its pale yellowness. Instead, it flushed red as he lifted his five-pound weights. Deryk had moved Jack's eating table so he could exercise comfortably in his recording room rather than his bedroom. The orange backdrop had become a staple on his channel.

"*One more,*" Jack puffed, curling both his arms toward himself. He felt every part of his body burning. The heater being on full blast only added to the pool of sweat he sat in.

Deryk had suggested they get Jack out of his chair. Jack wanted to do so but on camera. Deryk declined to be on camera, so Jack decided to try it out on his own. While Deryk stood by, Jack recorded a video.

He sat in his chair, waving to the camera, then he planted both hands onto the armrests and pushed. His foot reached out toward the floor, like a hand grasping for help, and slowly Jack inched his way from his chair like a snail without its shell. His arms trembled, jiggling his entire body, but his foot planted onto the ground firmly. Putting his weight onto it, he felt the muscles constrict painfully. He lifted his other foot, still covered in a neon green cast, and quickly planted it down beside the other, refraining from putting most of the weight on it. His face had contorted into painful expressions, but there he stood, holding his chair for support. He looked at the camera and smiled, letting go of the chair. For a moment he tottered, like a baby taking their first steps, and then he was as still as a statue, waving at his audience.

He edited this into a short video and posted it, racking up views quickly. There were the people who congratulated him, the people who condemned him for his weight, and the old fans who hated his new content. He was happy with his small bits of progress and decided to do a live exercise video.

Deryk helped Jack back into his chair and retrieved the weights for him, and as Jack pumped his iron for a live audience, Deryk watched in awe.

He couldn't believe the rapidity of Jack's weight gain. It was incredible, but with as many videos as he'd made in the last three years and the thousands of pounds of food he must have consumed, it made it more believable.

He silently cheered Jack on from behind the camera, acting as his cheerleader. He convinced himself he would help Jack get to the point of self-preservation. No one would have to wait hand and foot on him anymore, and maybe his wife would return. Deryk had been put into these situations often, replacing an MIA spouse. Most times, he couldn't blame them despite what he'd been through. Marriage isn't a contract to take care of someone until they die. A person can only be stretched so thin. Deryk thought of an elderly woman he'd cared for years ago almost every night. Her dementia completely rotted her memory away, and every morning, she would fight her husband, believing she was a young girl in her parents' home, and he was an intruder trying to assault her. She would kick and scream and beat him. No matter how many photos he showed her of their wedding or their children, she would yell, "*You're a pervert. Get out of my room, you sick bastard!*"

The husband cried nightly, finally making the call to Deryk's company. He'd left the keys with Deryk and said, "I'll be back in a jiffy. I'm out to get a gallon of milk."

Jeffrey never returned while Silvia still breathed, but his bill was always paid on time.

One time Silvia asked about Jeffrey. Deryk had been sure he removed all the photos of the man from that house months after he left, but she'd found one.

She held it and said, "This man, he looks familiar. Why do I love him?"

Deryk had silently taken the photo from her hands and tucked it away, unsure of what to tell her. He stayed with her day and night as this had been before his own family, and they played pretend that she was once again eight years old. He was astonished to find out she had an uncle that looked like him, and she called Deryk *Uncle Rick*. She liked tea parties and singing her ABCs and reading story books. Her favorite color was pastel pink, and she'd convinced Deryk to paint her bedroom pink with white teddy bears. He did, and she loved it. And shortly after, Silvia passed.

Jeffrey somehow knew, as if he'd sensed it, and he showed up the next day. Deryk broke the news, but Jeffrey pushed it off. He screamed at Deryk for painting the walls of his house and told him to never come back again.

Deryk did not blame Jeffrey for leaving, and he did not blame Silvia for hurting Jeffrey on so many occasions. Some situations in life are blameless, and one can only try to right what is wrong without bias.

He didn't blame Mia for leaving, but he could blame Jack for his choices in life. He couldn't wrap his mind around it all. The fame was there; they just had to adapt. Now this man was incapable of taking care of himself and his attitude had grown as much as his ass.

"Alright! I think that's enough for today! My new nur— trainer has been telling me that for people like me, it's best to take it slow. I need to *listen to my body*, and my body is saying *we are done!*"

Deryk tapped the recording button, shutting down the live stream.

"How do you think I did?" Jack asked, looking up at Deryk with a smile.

"I think you did great! And I think tomorrow it'll be even easier." He unclipped the phone and handed it to Jack. Jack scanned through the comments.

Fat ass.

Waste of life.

DISGUSTING.

Jack's smile faded.

"What's the matter, buddy?" Deryk asked, resting a hand on Jack's shoulder.

"*Don't touch me.*" Jack thought back to the night before, about Rochelle's words. He glared up at Deryk. "You're only doing this because it's your job."

Deryk was hurt. No matter the number of times he heard the phrase, it still stung the same each time, "Jack." He put his hands on his hips, thinking. "Jack, I created this business myself. I employ other nurses, but before that it was just me. A lone nurse staying at people's bedsides when hospitals had abandoned them. I don't care because I do this. I do this because I care, Jack."

They held eye contact for a minute before Jack's mouth stretched in a deep, open frown and he mewled. "*I miss Mia!*" He sobbed, clutching at Deryk's arm and bringing it to his face. Deryk put his other arm around Jack's shoulder.

"It'll be okay. She'll come back."

"But—but I can't figure it out."

"Figure what out?"

"*Myself.* I can't figure out why I'm so mean."

The pain in Jack's voice gripped Deryk's heart. "Well, buddy, even if you treat me like yesterday's trash, I'll still be here, quietly giving you care and support."

Jack squeezed Deryk's arm tighter. "I just miss her so much, Deryk."

He looked down at the top of Jack's shiny head. "Why do you miss her?"

"Well, she's my wife."

"Yeah, but other than that? What would you do if she were here?"

"Cry and hug her."

Deryk shook his head. "Like a child missing his mama."

"Well, what would you do?" Jack sniveled, swallowing a glob of mucus.

"Well, my baby mama left me and my daughter when my daughter was born. I was a single dad for a long time. I didn't cry for her to come back. I cried because my daughter didn't have a woman in her life. My sister tried to be a mom, but then I met Trisha, and she's taken better care of my daughter than any other woman could. If she left me, well, I might cry in private, but to her face, I would apologize and offer her the world."

"You wouldn't get down on your knees and cry for her to come back?"

"Nah, that's some kid stuff. That's what five-year-olds do when you threaten to take away their favorite toy, and women aren't toys."

Jack silently nodded.

Mia threw herself onto the bed, listening to it creak under her weight. She'd driven too many hours, her thoughts the only thing keeping her from veering off the road with closed eyes. The smell of must emanated around her, but her mind blocked it out. It even blocked out the way the sheets felt crusty under her fingers and the way the pillowcase prickled into her cheek.

Her eyes closed, her body relaxing into the bed, and that's when the music started.

A thumping from next door followed by clinking glass and hoots opened her eyes. She sat up on the edge of the mattress, wishing the bed could have just been put against the other wall. Sighing, she got up and went to the door. She grabbed the door handle, steadying herself with a deep breath.

Outside, a chill breeze met her before she rapped her knuckles against the door of her temporary neighbor. A young man answered the door, a beer in hand. He smirked, about to speak when Mia cut him off.

"Hey, could you guys turn it down a bit? I'm really sorry but it's just—I haven't slept all night. I've been on the road—"

The man laughed, soon followed by a group of young men his age scattered about the hotel room. "Oh, hey, guys, looks like we gotta turn it down for this ol' hooker over here." The room erupted in louder laughter.

"Maybe you should sleep at night instead of spreading your legs!" a man called from the corner of the room.

Another one called, *"Whore!"*

Mia's attention went back to the young man who answered the door. He pouted his lips and pushed his chest together, shimmying from side to side as the other men giggled. The man laughed.

The little voice in the back of her head whispered, *Hit him.*

Mia balled up her fist and struck him in the nose. Blood sprayed freely as her knuckles caved into his face. He stumbled backwards.

Mia spoke under her breath, *"Fuck you."*

A girl from the back of the room made her way through the crowd, cussing. She shoved Mia backward, out onto the balcony which overlooked the parking lot. Mia reached into her pocket, retrieving a switchblade. She pressed the button, the *flick* of the blade causing the girl's eyes to widen.

"You wanna die today? *Because I'm ready to fucking kill!*" Mia bared her teeth and slashed toward the girl.

She barely dodged it, as people inside called to her.

"Get back inside!"

"Fuck her!"

"Crazy crackhead!"

The girl ran inside, slamming the door shut.

Mia walked back to her room, the switchblade still in her hand. She threw it on the floor beside the bed and fell into the itchy sheets. The music subsided until she heard the entire group leave, and her eyes gently closed. She figured the group was underage and drinking, hence their disinterest in calling the police.

Her body trembled, muscles twitching here and there. Tears seeped from her closed eyes, soaking the pillow under her. She sobbed into it, tasting salt, until she fell asleep.

Jack's tongue salivated as salt and sweetness danced on it. Before him, a large watermelon that he'd broken open with a mallet dripped onto the table. His lights and camera were on, centering him into the spotlight of his live audience as he chewed a slice of watermelon down to the rind. He'd sprinkled salt onto it, something he was sure to warn his audience about.

"Careful with the salt, lovelies! Especially those of you with high blood pressure."

Comments filtered in questioning his authority on *health*.

His old ways set in again as Jack snatched up a large piece. He licked the tip of it before sticking it in his mouth and taking a large, wet bite. Juice sprayed out from his lips, and he gave a small moan. He looked over, realizing it wasn't his wife by his side anymore. Deryk had been cringing, but quickly covered it with a smile and a thumbs up. Jack sighed, looking back at the camera.

"You know, guys, before I started my mukbang videos, I was *super* into the gym and eating right. Sometimes you get blinded by the things you want and end up regretting it."

Deryk stared at him with wide eyes.

He didn't do his baby voice.

People took note of this in the comments, but Jack had had enough.

"I'd like to thank today's sponsor for sending me watermelons and cantaloupes instead of the usual candied fruit. I'm so glad my sponsors have been able to adapt with me as I make this change."

Commenters went crazy over the lack of baby voice, much to Jack's discontent. He ate another slice before addressing it.

"I'd like to think my viewers would be happy with this change and be understanding of all the other changes I'm going to have to make in my life."

The views had dropped tremendously since Jack began his exercise videos, but his eating videos still gained a good amount. This one had started off strong, only to falter as people left.

No baby voice?? F that!

Aw, baby Jack's all grown up [eye roll emoji]

Jack shook his head and continued munching on the watermelon.

These people are impossible to please, he thought.

He chewed and slurped loudly for the camera, eating the entire watermelon until only the rind sat in front of him.

"Well, thanks for joining me, guys!"

Deryk rushed over and handed Jack the phone so he could end the live stream. Jack was shaking his head.

"What's the matter?"

"People hate me now, Deryk."

"Oh, they don't hate you."

"Yeah, they do! I don't get nearly the views I used to—or the comments."

"Well, the internet is a mutual ground for millions of people to interact, and most people don't want to see someone improving themselves. They want to watch someone destroy themselves just for the audience."

Jack nodded.

I wonder how much money a person could make committing suicide on a live stream.

He pushed that thought away. "Do you think I could take a nap, Deryk? I'm exhausted."

Deryk mulled it over, pushing his lips out. "Mmm, you think you could stay awake?"

Jack looked at him questioningly. "Why?"

"Well, taking naps could be why you can't sleep at night."

"Fine, I'll stay up." He pressed the lever on his chair to roll him out of the room. "But there isn't much to do up here."

Jack rolled into his bedroom and grabbed the TV remote. He clicked around through the same streaming services, which offered the same shows all the time, finally landing on an old cartoon. Old cartoons were Jack's favorite. He found them easily digestible and could shut his brain off while watching them.

He figured he ought to have asked Deryk to help him into bed. His chair was comfortable but not *watch TV* comfortable. He sat there, falling asleep until he remembered he had something *special* in his nightstand.

His eyes shifted to the door and back to the drawer. He opened it slowly, cautious to be quiet, and reached in. Out he pulled a long, slender silhouette into the dim room. His mouth salivated at the sight of the large candy bar. He pinched at the corner of the wrapper carefully and pulled down, cringing at the slight crinkling sound it made. Jack pulled the rest of the wrapper back, exposing chocolate-covered peanuts, caramel, and cookie. His lips wrapped around the bar and he sunk his teeth in. The sweet flavors melted on his tongue, immediately alleviating the headache he had. His skin prickled as he chewed, and all felt right.

As he gnashed the caramel and peanuts between his yellowed molars, Jack took another bite, smiling as the cookie crunched under his front teeth.

Deryk stepped into the doorway, and Jack jumped, throwing the candy bar onto the floor.

"I promise I was—I was going to throw that up." Jack trembled like a child under an unforgiving mother's gaze.

Deryk stared at him, wide-eyed. "Jack, it's okay to eat candy."

"It—" Jack looked at the candy bar on the floor and back to Deryk. "It is?"

"Yeah, you don't want to start a diet too quickly where the brain can't comprehend what's going on. You're still going to have cravings. And no matter how many *alternatives* you might try, nothing really hits the spot like the actual thing. You did really good today. And there's nothing wrong with one candy bar."

Jack sighed.

"See, your problem, Jack, is that you overeat. Even healthy foods, when you consume too much, will add up to too many calories."

Jack nodded, wishing he hadn't thrown his candy bar.

"I'll go grab you one from downstairs."

Ding-dong.

Jack's heart fluttered.

Could it really be Mia?

Why would she use the doorbell?

"You expecting anybody?" Deryk asked as he strolled down the hall.

"Oh my God," Jack said under his breath.

Rochelle.

"Yes!" he called. At no point in his recent life did he want to get up and out of his chair more than he did at that moment. He wanted to greet her at the door so graciously. To give her a hug and maybe even a kiss on the cheek. She had the perfect timing, almost like an angel, he thought.

Deryk opened the door, greeted with a bloodied Hispanic woman holding nothing more than a small purse on a chain. Out in the driveway sat a filthy beater, one of the headlights being busted.

"You must be Deryk," she said, tonelessly. She extended a hand, which Deryk did not take.

He closed the door and called, "*What's this girl's name?*"

"Rochelle! You can let her in."

He opened the door to a very angry Rochelle. She'd crossed her arms across her chest and was about to speak when Deryk held up a finger. "What's your name?"

"Rochelle."

Deryk stepped aside. "He's upstairs, but..." he trailed off as Rochelle pushed past him and to the staircase. She smelled ripely of bodily fluids. He quickly followed her, and when he entered Jack's bedroom, she was bent down hugging Jack. He held her tightly with his eyes closed. Deryk cleared his throat, and Jack quickly opened his eyes and let go.

"Deryk, this is Rochelle, she's—"

"She's covered in blood, Jack."

Rochelle blushed. "*Oh*, I had a bloody nose in the car. I'm so sorry. I didn't have anything else to change into."

Deryk didn't believe her. The way the stains seemed to only sweep across her sideways indicated more than a bloody nose, but he kept his mouth shut.

"She's my internet friend." Jack beamed.

Deryk nodded. "Ah, okay, well, I'll leave you to it."

As soon as Deryk left the room, he heard the door click shut behind him. Shaking his head, he made his way downstairs to wrap up the shopping list.

Rochelle sauntered her way back to Jack, reaching a hand from his shoulder to his neck with delicate fingers. She tickled the back of his bald head, traces of sweat wetting the tips of her fingers. Gripping the back of his head, she drew him closer, staring deeply into his eyes.

It was all Jack had ever wanted with her, yet the only thing on his mind was how dangerous the drive back to North Carolina was. He tried to fend it off but found himself cringing at her touch.

She didn't seem to notice as she raised her leg to sit in his lap. Her butt cheek grazed his knee and that's when his arms shot out. The palms of his hands struck her shoulder and arm, sending her to the floor in a heap.

Had it not been out of pure fear, Jack didn't think he could ever move so fast. Rochelle looked up to him from the floor, her eyes blazing.

"*What the fuck, Jack?*"

Jack's eyebrows furrowed, and he was unsure what to say. "Mia—"

"Yeah, Mia left your ass!" She stood up, rubbing the butt cheek she landed on.

"Well, yeah." Jack shrugged.

"Yeah, and I'm just offering you comfort. Physical touch is important to humans." She threw her hands up in disbelief. "Or was all the stuff you said online a lie?"

"No." Jack shook his head, so terribly afraid she was going to leave him, too. "No, I'm just not ready."

"You were ready when she was here. Why aren't you ready now that she's gone?"

Jack's eyes filled with tears, and his voice shook when he said, "*I don't know!*"

"*I came all this way, Jack! All this way to see you and be held by you like you promised!*" She wrapped her arms around herself. "Unless that's not what you want." Her large, round eyes wetted with tears and her lower lip pouted outward slightly.

Jack felt something within himself snap. "*Two years of my life spent trying to please you fucks and all you can do is ask me for more!*" His face reddened with the force of his booming voice. "*Two years of gorging myself for your pleasure and now you want to fuck me as soon as you meet me like I'm some doll! Like my existence is only to please you! I'm just Rochelle's fucking entertainment, I guess!*"

Rochelle's eyes widened, and rather than tears, a string of words flew out of her. "*You did this to yourself, you asshole! I never asked you to 'gorge yourself' on camera, and I didn't ask for you to sext me every night!*"

Deryk swung open the door with the force of a bull, the spring door stopper slamming into the baseboard. He snatched Rochelle's arm and dragged her out of the room. Rochelle screamed and tried to pull away, but when Deryk looked back at her and seemed to stare into her soul, she quieted and walked with him.

This left Jack alone in his room, a sniveling mess. He scooted over to his bed and snatched up his phone. His thumb hovered over her contact photo for quite some time. It was a candid photo of Mia in a shop in Mexico. In it she wore a traditional Huipil. He remembered the shop owner begged Mia to try it on and take a photo so she could hang it on her wall.

Jack pressed the call button.

The wind blew her hair into a flailing mess, but she didn't mind. The heater had made the car too warm and damp feeling, just like the house she'd left. Jack's photo came up on her phone, and his ringtone blared throughout the car.

This motherfucker.

Nothing but red rock surrounded the car on a desolate strip of asphalt through Utah. The sun beat down on the rear of the car but brought with it no warmth. She stomped the gas, climbing from seventy-five to seventy-nine miles-per-hour.

I hope he's gotten himself stuck in the bathtub. Yeah, he decided to take a little snack into that poor tub and before he knew it, he was sticking to the sides. Now, he's barely able to breathe and thought he'd call me.

She laughed and shook her head, knowing damn well that wasn't the case.

Maybe he rolled his scooter to the edge of the stairs.

Mia cackled as she thought about that plump man rolling down the stairs like a blob of slime.

Bam. Bam. Bam.

She imagined his head smacking each stair as he tumbled over it.

And there at the bottom of the stairs he would lie sprawled out, bleeding profusely from the back of his head and nose like he should have the night he fell.

She nodded.

I'd like to see that.

She pressed the gas a little harder, the needle now climbing past ninety. Her shiny black car shot across the freeway like a bullet. A lone, fiery bullet.

Jack's ringer finally ended, and his photo stopped staring at her from the cupholder. She accelerated more, feeling the way her car cut through the air, and the needle pushed one hundred.

Jack wailed.

Deryk could hear him from downstairs.

"*He doesn't need you,*" Rochelle hissed.

"Oh, and he needs you? You could cause him to have a heart attack. He's going through enough right now and he doesn't need *you.*" He thrust a finger in her face, seething.

"Who the fuck are you anyway? You're just paid to pretend to care."

"I'm all he's got right now."

"I'm here."

Deryk scoffed. "Yeah, well, I'm the only stable thing in his life right now, so unless you start cooking for him, bathing him, cleaning up after him, helping him in and out of bed, and helping him on and off the toilet then you better *shut the fuck up*."

"*Deryk!*" Jack called.

Deryk spun around to go up the stairs, and with his foot on the first stair he looked back at Rochelle. "*Duty calls*."

As he bound up the stairs, Rochelle followed at his heels but had to stop when Deryk slammed the door in her face. He leaned against the door, his entire body vibrating as she pounded her fist on the wood.

"What do I do, Deryk?" Jack asked from behind his hands. Tears dripped down his wrists and onto his bare chest.

Deryk leaned all his weight against the door as Rochelle twisted the handle and forced her own weight onto it. "Honestly, I don't like Rochelle, and since Mia is gone, I think you should focus on yourself right now. I don't think you need Rochelle here getting in the way of your progress."

"*Fucker!*" she screamed from the other side of the door.

"Yeah," Jack hiccuped, "but she's been so nice to me. I think I should let her stay."

"You really—"

"*She doesn't have anything or anyone else, Deryk.*"

The banging on the door ceased as Rochelle listened.

"I'm just thinking about your health, Jack."

"Well, part of being healthy is being happy, and I think she should stick around. I just," he sighed, "I just need time."

"I'm not cooking or cleaning for her. Mia hired me to take care of you. *Not* your mistress."

"Mistress?!" Jack was startled out of his tears.

"Yeah, *Jack*, Rochelle is a mistress."

"She's a *friend*."

"A friend that's trying to fuck the instant she meets you is still a mistress."

"Mia's the one that left *me. I* didn't leave her."

"And I don't blame her."

Jack's face scrunched, and he wailed again.

"Jesus Christ, Jack."

Rochelle began to beat the door again.

"I support that you're working on changing yourself, but you're not a very nice person."

"*Let me in!*"

Deryk reached back, flicking the lock over so Rochelle couldn't open the door, and walked over to Jack. He bent over and hugged him around the shoulders, careful to keep his face from touching Jack's sticky skin.

"We're going to get through this together."

"Okay."

Rochelle and Jack sat across from each other, and between them was a roasted chicken—the kind they set out at grocery stores in plastic containers. Deryk sat at the end of the table, as far away from the couple as possible, with his hand supporting his chin. Dinner had been quiet as Rochelle intently stared at Jack as he ripped through most of the chicken with his bare hands. Deryk was glad he served himself and Rochelle first. He was tired and bored, sitting at the table like a child in school.

Had it been a more advanced dinner, he wouldn't have offered Rochelle anything, but after her shower and change of clothes, she looked exhausted, and he felt for the girl. If what Jack said was true, she didn't have anything in this world besides the body she was in, the purse she carried, and the bloody clothes she had walked in wearing. Not to mention her beat up car, but Deryk didn't think it had much time left in it.

It had been a long time since Jack had a meal that wasn't on camera. He hadn't had a meal, or even a snack, with Mia in months, maybe even a year, and he did appreciate Rochelle and Deryk's presence more than he could say. Still, Mia was the only one on his mind.

The chicken tasted bland as he shoveled in chunks and strips of the white meat, and he thought of all the ways Mia was spending her day.

Driving on the freeway, hopefully safely. Hopefully not overturned in a ditch or drowning in a lake, submerged in her car. I hope she hasn't found the front end of a semi or a locomotive.

What if she's pulled over and broke down? And a man comes by to help her, only to kidnap her...

He dipped a piece of chicken into the bowl of gravy next to his soda and shoved it into his mouth. Faintly, Jack remembered the taste of chicken with gravy, but he only tasted oil in his mouth.

Jack swallowed and said, "I think we should be friends, Rochelle." He gave her an awkward, closed-mouth smile.

In return, she gave him a glare. "What does that mean?"

"I just want to set some boundaries. I like you, but I need time."

Deryk watched, finally cured of his boredom. His eyes bounced back and forth as if he was at a tennis match.

"Time for what?"

Jack shrugged. "Time to heal—I don't know? This all happened so fast."

"And didn't you just ask Mia to have a baby?" Deryk asked. If anything, he only wanted to stir the pot. He was stuck there for a few more hours.

"You *what?*"

"I—I asked if she'd like to have a baby, and then she left." Jack looked down at the chicken and pushed it away.

"And she left you like that?"

He nodded.

"You shouldn't want to have a baby with her," she said matter-of-factly. She sat up straight in her seat, pointing her nose up. "I'm younger."

"What are you insinuating?" Jack shook his head, rubbing his temples with his eyes closed. They popped open, and he asked, "What are you saying?"

"My body's plumper and more prepared for a child."

Jack scoffed. "I also *barely* know you."

"*You said you'd fuck me the second day we started talking!*" She slammed her hands onto the table, jarring everyone's meals.

115

"Texting is one thing!" Then a thought came to him.

I haven't reached the Hispanic community before…

And people would love *her looks. Mia's pretty, but Rochelle is a* different *type of pretty.*

She could name the baby something traditional to where she's from and people would die *over it.*

The table was silent for a few minutes before Jack spoke up.

"I'll think about it."

"Well, I'm headed out for the night," Deryk said, peeking his head into Jack's recording room where he'd just cleared out the dishes.

Rochelle sat close to Jack, and by the smile on Jack's face he seemed relieved to see Deryk.

But the smile faded when he asked, "What about my bath?"

Deryk thought to himself, *This man can't get much more selfish, can he?*

"We'll do that tomorrow. Your skin needs time to adjust to washing it. If I wash you tonight, I guarantee you, you'll be sore and itchy tomorrow."

Jack nodded, his face suddenly solemn. "Okay, I'll see you tomorrow."

"See you tomorrow, Jack. I'll be sure to lock the place up on my way out."

Jack nodded and looked back at Rochelle. Without makeup on, his original ten out of ten rating went to a seven.

She smiled softly at him and asked, "Can we go to the bedroom?"

Of all the nights he'd dreamed she'd ask that, he didn't so much want to at the moment. He wanted to know if Mia was okay, despite his feelings that she'd let him down. But he agreed, wheeling his chair in behind her.

She plopped down into his bed, in the same place Mia used to lay before his body took up most of the mattress.

"Aren't you going to help me into bed?" he asked.

Rochelle's smile faltered, but she restored it before Jack noticed. She got up and stood next to Jack, looking down at the way his body bulged outward.

"What," she paused, looking up at the hoists, "what do I do?"

Jack sighed. "You lower that handle there."

"How?"

"Press the button there and pull. When you release it, it stays in place."

"Okay." Rochelle did so.

"Okay, I'll take that." Jack took the handle and pressed the button, zapping the slack back into the hoist. "So, I'll pull myself up as you pick me up."

"Pick you up?"

"Yep."

Jack's face contorted and instantly reddened as he strained to pull his weight out of his chair. Rochelle moved her hands to his side, then to his back, then to his other side.

"I—I don't know where to grab."

Jack grunted, "Under my armpits."

Rochelle slipped her fingers into the doughy flesh of Jack's underarms and lifted.

Jack pulled harder, getting some of his weight out of the seat. "*Push!*"

Rochelle shoved up and toward the bed, her fingers slick with Jack's sweat. He threw himself onto the mattress, using that momentum to roll toward the middle, and proceeded to inch his way toward the headboard. Rochelle watched as the tip of his bald head hit the wood. Jack flipped himself over, groaning loudly, and wiggled up into a sitting position.

"Mia usually puts me closer to the headboard, but you'll get the hang of it," he said, smiling.

Rochelle took a deep breath, her back burning from the effort, and plopped onto the foot of the bed near Jack's feet. She looked down at them as he used his toes to take off his socks. With toenails like yellowed clam shells, it was no wonder he could take his socks off with ease. Rochelle turned away and went to rub her eye when she was assaulted with a foul odor. First thinking it was Jack's feet, she looked down at them, but when her finger was an inch from her eye, the smell became unbearable. She looked down at it and sniffed, revulsion contorting her face.

Jack didn't notice as he checked his phone. He went to Mia's chat, their last conversation going:

Jack: *Did you forget to buy gallons of milk?*

Mia: *No.*

Jack: *Then bring them up.*

He sighed, typing out: *I hope you're okay. Love you.*

Jack desperately wanted to erase it, but more than anything he wished she'd never left, so he sent it and waited.

"Who are you texting?" Rochelle asked, slinking over on her hands and knees. She slyly wiped her fingers on the sheets, smearing the cheesy smell deep into them as she crawled over.

"Mia," Jack said, looking at her contact photo.

Rochelle sat propped up next to him on the small sliver of bed leftover and looked over his shoulder at his phone.

"She's so pretty," she said, shaking her head.

I knew I couldn't compete.

"You think so?" Jack asked, looking at Rochelle.

"Well, yeah. She was a model." She scratched her arm. "I could never be a model."

"Why do you say that?" Jack reached out and touched Rochelle's forearm.

"Look at Mia. She's so skinny, and her figure is sleek and like—like a goddess." She looked away from the photo. "I could never be like her."

"You don't have to, Rochelle." She turned to face him, seeing a warm smile on his face. "Aphrodite is depicted with meat on her bones. She's curvy and beautiful and full of love, just like you." He shrugged. "Mia got into modeling very young. She's always on strict diets and exercise regimens. It's honestly no fun." He lightly laughed. "You, on the other hand, you're not tied down to almost religious practices for your body, and your curves are beautiful."

"Yeah?"

Her dark brown eyes enveloped him, just like Mia's used to. "Yes. Mia is beautiful, and you are beautiful."

She sighed and leaned against him. Jack put his arm around her shoulders, airing out more of that smell. Rochelle didn't mind because she finally felt warm.

She smirked a little, thinking of how easily she changed the topic on his mind, and Jack smirked a little, thinking of how viral their mixed child was going to be, whether he had a child with Rochelle or Mia.

Chapter Eight: A Scarred Weiner

Snow beat across the windshield faster than the wipers could keep up, and Mia kept her eyes peeled for red lights or, God forbid, headlights. With few other cars on the road, Mia had little to keep her focus sharp. The asphalt before her car steadily swept under it until flurries of snow fell from the sky. She'd tried the radio, from talk shows to country to rap to pop, and she couldn't find anything that didn't irk her.

"This is K21 radio playing YOUR favorites from the 2000s and more!"

She'd snapped it off at the start of a song she loathed and drove in silence. Her phone had been beckoning, its dark screen facing her like a blank face. She finally gave in, watching the road as she felt around for her phone. She picked it up and held it up so she could see the road and her phone at once. Her mother's contact photo came up, an old picture of her holding Mia long ago in the kitchen of their restaurant. She hit the call button and waited.

The road passed by, humming under her as the phone rang and rang. She shook her head, tears blurring her vision.

They're dead. I know it.

Ding.

A text message from Jack came in. Mia grunted, swiping it aside while not looking at the road. A patch of ice, large enough to have been seen and small enough to have been swerved around, swept under her tire. The steering wheel twisted, and Mia overcorrected, her phone falling onto the weather mat at her feet. Her car turned sideways on the highway, and she spun a full U-turn before hitting another patch of ice. With no snow chains, the car slid off the road.

Mia screamed, gripping the wheel with white-knuckled hands as she pulled it to the right. Meanwhile, the car slid to the left, slamming into an embankment of snow.

She'd let off the brakes and gas long ago, and sitting there, catching her breath, she put the car into park. Mia screamed, tears flowing down her cheeks. Violently, she twisted the key, shutting the car off. She put her arms up onto the steering wheel and buried her face, sobbing and trembling. Her face contorted painfully as she let everything out in hot tears that wetted her shoes.

When she looked up, snow blanketed the windshield, giving her a blank, white view. She looked down, noticing her phone by her foot. Picking it up, she tried the power button.

Nothing.

She gasped, pressing the button over and over.

Where is my phone charger?

Mia's mind played the memory of her slipping it into her last suitcase, the one in the trunk. With how fast the snow was coming down, she knew everything in the trunk would be soaked if she went out and looked for it. She sighed and tried the key.

The car made a grinding noise, and Mia pulled the key back.

Fuck.

She tried again, this time only met with a click. She shook her head, pulling out the key and looking at it. It appeared fine, so she put it in a third time.

Third time's the charm, right?

Nothing.

"*No!*" she said, punching her steering wheel.

Mia sat, thinking for a few minutes as the cold seeped into her car. Her only solution was out in the abysmal snowstorm on the other side of her car door.

Shaking, she slid over to the passenger seat, her side having been barricaded by snow. Having no way of seeing, she hoped there were no cars coming to swoop her door off as she opened it. She clambered out into the snow, the chill instantly eating through her sneakers, sweatpants, and sweatshirt, and slammed the door shut, keys in hand.

The wind sliced against her cheek, throwing snowflakes into her eyelashes and hair. She stomped over ice and snow toward the road, of which she'd only slid off a car's width. Squinting her eyes to shield them from the cold, she hoped to see headlights. Her foot crossed over the fog line, and the other followed suit.

Soon, she was standing in the middle of a highway in Wyoming as a snowstorm raged around her. She buried her hands deep into her pockets, gripping her thighs for warmth and bouncing from foot to foot.

If only I hadn't buried the fucking flares under all my bags.

She shook her head, thinking of the disgustingly hot house she'd left and the way the moisture inside clung to her body at all times.

I will stand here and freeze before going back to that house.

Two white dots slowly grew larger in the distance. Mia didn't know whether she should stay in the middle of the road or move off to the side with her car. She could imagine them rolling right by as she waved from next to her car, but she could also imagine how her entrails would steam on the snowy road after impact.

Yet she remained on the road, her feet straddling the yellow, broken line.

The headlights approached closer, and Mia thought they must have been moving along slowly in the lane closest to where her car had left her stranded.

Her toes and fingers felt numb, and she hoped the car would stop for her. As it came closer, she noticed how tall it was, figuring it to be a truck, and before she knew it, it was only a hundred yards before her. It barreled toward her, and as she finally saw a figure behind the wheel, they blared their horn. She frantically waved her arms and jumped, hoping they would at least slow down.

They didn't.

Mia moved over into the middle of the lane that they drove in and waved harder. She figured she must have looked ridiculous when she heard something squealing. Looking into the cab, she could see the driver waving her away, but the red glow behind the truck indicated they had hit their brakes.

But they aren't slowing down.

A shiver flew up her spine as she realized the truck was skidding toward her, now veering sideways, she remained in its path. She ran toward the center lane as the truck ran her down. Even if she were to make it there in a few steps, the truck was only twenty feet away and sliding sideways, taking up both lanes. She leapt, throwing herself into the median and landing harshly. She gasped and quickly crawled forward.

The truck flew past her, the driver still on the horn and staring at Mia in the median.

She scrambled to her feet, panting as she watched the truck finally slow to a stop. She ran over, almost certain she was about to get a fist to her jaw, but equally desperate to get out of the cold.

The driver swung the truck around to face the right direction and parked on the side of the road, a few bus lengths ahead of Mia's car. He busted out of his truck, screaming.

"*What the fuck are you doing in the middle of the road, you son of a bitch?!*"

Mia raised her hands and showed her palms to the man in a gesture of helplessness. "My car broke down!" she yelled, having slowed her pace toward him to a walk.

He approached hot and fast, his angry eyes peeking out from under his beanie. Pointing at her with a gloved hand, he yelled, "*You could have killed us both!*"

"*I'm sorry!*" she screamed. She kept her hands raised, on the verge of tears again. "*I'm sorry,*" she muttered under her breath, looking down at her cold feet.

The older man's face softened, and he slowly lowered his accusing hand. He approached Mia, and she looked up at him, unsure if she should back away. His hand gently cupped her elbow, and he said, "Get out of the road, Miss."

They walked over to his truck, which still puffed out clouds of exhaust into the chill air, and he pulled a cigarette carton out of his pocket along with a lighter. He selected one from the box and lit it, cupping his hands to guard the lighter's flame. Mia watched in silence, the tips of her fingers aching.

"You want one?"

The smell reminded Mia of her childhood. She'd sit out back of the restaurant and smoke cigarettes she and her friends had gotten older guys to buy them. They'd laugh and cough and giggle some more until her parents came looking for her.

She shook her head. "No, thank you."

"Smart girl," he said, tucking away the pack. He stuck the cigarette between his lips and stuffed his hands in his pockets as he started for Mia's car. "So, how long have you been out here?"

"I actually just slid off the road probably twenty minutes ago."

"Twenty minutes is a long time in the cold." He pulled the cigarette from between his lips and coughed. It was a hearty smoker's cough that made Mia's lungs burn just from hearing it. "Did it shut off when you smacked the snowbank?"

"No, I shut it off and now it won't start."

"Ah," he said, trudging through the snow behind Mia's car. He looked down at the license plate. "Typical Californian mistake."

Mia laughed. She wasn't sure why she laughed when he was clearly making a joke about her intelligence, but it was funny, nonetheless. "I'm actually from North Carolina."

"Stole the car?"

"No," she paused, laughing again, "No, I moved out to California a while ago, but I grew up in North Carolina."

"Ah." He walked around to the front end. "Get in and pop the hood."

Mia got in the passenger side and leaned over the center console to pull the lever that would pop her hood. The door was still open, her knee resting on the passenger side, and her butt sticking part way out the door.

A shiver went up her spine as she imagined the man coming up behind her and grabbing her, maybe even pulling her into his hips. Mia scrambled out of the car, seeing that the man was leaned over her engine compartment, checking the oil.

"Well, seems like everything is okay in here," he said with a smile.

"How come it won't start?" She was ashamed for her thoughts, but out on a desolate highway in the middle of a snowstorm, she couldn't help but feel paranoid that the only person within a mile of her was a man she'd just met.

"Your battery is a couple years old, and the cold really sucks the life out of them."

"Okay," she responded, unsure where to go from there.

"I'll give you a jump. It's too bad you didn't slip off the road two miles ahead. There's an exit with a hotel right up there."

Mia shook her head. "It's just my luck."

"Yeah, or could be that you should have changed out your battery." He laughed, coughing afterward. "I'll go get my truck. You keep an eye out for traffic."

Mia watched for traffic as he got in his truck and drove the wrong way to come park in front of her car which was facing the wrong way as well. He spun around, nosed his truck up to the car, and got out. When he grabbed a shovel from the bed of his truck, Mia looked at him questioningly.

He chuckled. "No point in starting the thing if it's buried in a couple hundred pounds of snow. Here," he handed Mia the shovel, "start scraping away at the snow on your roof." He went back to his truck and retrieved another shovel as Mia gently scraped small bits of snow away.

"You ain't going to get anywhere like that!" he said from the front end of her car. He slammed the hood closed. "Jeez," he shook his head. "One: you're lucky only the ass end of the thing is stuck in a bit of snow and not the whole side. Two: you're lucky this snow just fell, cuz otherwise it would've been like smacking into a brick wall." He jammed the shovel into the snow above her wheel well and tore a chunk free.

Mia watched in awe as he chipped away at the snow, carving out a section so her tire could move. She tried to emulate him but was terrified of scratching the roof of her car. Shortly, he came over and scooted her out of the way.

"You gotta put your back into it, girly."

Mia watched this total stranger free her car from the snow. He took the shovel from her and threw them both in the back of his truck, then got into the cab and retrieved a small plastic box. Almost slipping, he made it to the front end of her car. He wiggled the lever of her partially open hood, lifted it, and propped it open. Mia watched as he hooked up a red and black cable to her battery.

"What if your truck doesn't jumpstart my car?" she asked as he went around to the cab of his truck and popped the hood.

He laughed loudly, standing at the front end of his truck, fingering the latch, and let his hood open on its own. "*I* just changed my battery last month to prepare for winter." He slung his leg up onto the tire and leaned into the engine compartment, fiddling around with the caps on his battery studs.

Mia watched, wondering how he wasn't afraid the hood would fall on him. She figured with how large it was, it must be heavy, and if it fell on him, it would surely chew him up in the steadily moving engine. She jumped when he hopped off the tire and landed on the icy asphalt.

"Alright, you get in, and when I rev up my truck, you start your car."

"But it won't start."

He looked at her with wide eyes and shook his head. "Well, then you turn the key like you're going to start it."

Mia got into her car, wishing she'd have taken mechanics class in high school instead of ceramics.

When was the last time I even made a mug or pot? she thought, waiting for him to rev up his truck.

When she heard the exhaust bellow from her passenger door, she quickly turned the key. The car wined a bit before starting up. Mia gasped and scrambled out of the car.

With triumphant arms high in the air, she said, "We did it!" as he walked over.

He unhooked the cables from both her car and his truck and wound them up, tucking them into their plastic case.

"Now, *do not* shut your car off until you get to a safe place. It *will* not start the next time."

"It won't?"

"Most likely. That battery ain't got much life to it, so be careful."

"Okay," Mia paused, fiddling with her hands in the front pocket of her sweatshirt. "Now, where did you say that motel is?"

He pointed down the road as if pointing directly at the motel itself. "Just down the road two miles, but the sign is going to be hard to see in the snow."

As he said it, Mia realized how much the storm had picked up. She'd been so focused on what this man was doing to even notice the inch of snow on the roof of her car.

"I can guide you down the road if you'd like," he said, shrugging.

"I—"

"Yeah, just follow my taillights, and I'll get you over there. You got insurance?"

She looked at him, furrowing her brow. "Why?"

"Oh, some places will deliver you a battery if you break down."

"Oh."

"Yeah. If not, I know there's a place in town not too far from the hotel."

"Yeah, that'd be great. If you can give me the address, I can call a taxi."

"Ah, I can drive you over there. Free of charge." He smiled at her, his blackened gums reminding her of the flesh underneath Jack's rolls and in all the places he wouldn't let her clean.

"Are—are you sure? You really don't have to."

"No worries at all." His smile remained fixed, surrounded by prickly, white hair that only filled in parts of his face in patches.

"Okay."

Mia got in her car as he got into his truck, and as she seated herself behind the wheel, thankful for the heater, she realized she hadn't even caught this man's name. Her windshield wipers painstakingly pushed aside the snow enough for her to see, and she watched as he passed her by with a wave. She scanned for traffic up ahead, which was actually behind. The sun had begun to set, and it was halfway to dusk, and Mia feared for her life.

She crept forward, turning her wheel and hoping she could make it in one pass. She didn't want to perform a three-point turn in the middle of a snow covered, dark freeway. The car made it around, slipping to the right a bit on some ice before straightening out.

Mia sighed deeply and looked ahead to the man's lights. Their red glow was her beacon of hope, and she felt terrible she didn't have more to offer the man in return.

I could give him my sneakers or a pair of sunglasses, she thought with a grin.

As she sped up, the snow tunneled around the windshield, and she found herself focused only on those red lights. She was so focused that when he turned on his blinker to get onto the exit, she jumped.

Slowing down was harder than speeding up, she realized as she hit the brake and continued behind him at the same speed. Mia's foot pumped the brake, pushing and releasing like she thought she was supposed to, and she gradually came to a full stop before continuing at a snail's pace.

He turned off the exit up ahead of her, and Mia scanned for headlights. She turned right and immediately had to turn into the hotel's parking lot. Following his truck, Mia parked at the back of the parking lot. The rest was mostly filled.

"Alright," he said, getting out of his truck as Mia opened her door. She locked her car and stood in between the two vehicles as he came around.

"Uh, you go ahead and get in. I'm gonna go see if they've got a pisser."

Mia nodded, thinking about his vocabulary. She opened the door and heaved herself into the truck. Without a step, she had to lift her leg high and rely on the handle above her head.

The smell of must hit her square in the face, tickling her eyes. The seat cover on the brown bench seat was rough and in an odd pattern.

Almost like pixelated UFOs?

Mia had never seen the pattern before and wondered where he'd gotten it. It scratched against her back, even through her sweatshirt. The dash was cooked, the material overlaying it crispy and peeling upward. Little flakes of it sat at her feet on the doormat that was coated in dirt and dry grass. Looking over, she could see wear marks from where this man sat. She figured he'd had this truck a long time or drove for long hours at a time every day. The steering wheel looked uncomfortable. Little cracks had formed on it, which were sure to poke into the driver's fingers. She shuddered, thinking of them dragging across her hand while making a turn. The glass was foggy, and she couldn't tell if it was from her breath in the cold or age. She'd seen old, abandoned vehicles whose glass had clouded over and wondered what they made windows out of back then.

He opened the door, startling Mia out of her thoughts. When he hopped in and saw the surprise on her face, he laughed.

"Didn't mean to startle you."

"Oh, no, sorry. I was just thinking." She looked down at her hands in her lap.

"Yeah, thinking about what?" he asked, an eyebrow raised.

"Ah, just how cold it is here."

He laughed again, finishing it off with a cough into his hand. "Yeah, winter here is rough. We can definitely always look forward to a *white* Christmas." He shook his head. "Damn snow caves in roofs and sheds and barns like it ain't *shit*."

Mia chuckled. "We get a bit of snow up where I live in California."

"Yeah?" He smiled, putting the truck into reverse. "What about a quarter of an inch per year?"

Mia laughed. "I think we got a foot in a week once, and I didn't even know what to do. That was when I first moved there."

"Yeah, California is weird." He backed out of the parking space and waited as another vehicle pulled into the lot.

"You've been?" she asked.

He put the truck into drive and crept out of the parking lot, turning right before saying, "Yeah, I travel a lot for work."

"Oh, yeah? What do you do?"

"I'm a welder."

And just like that, the twangy smell mingling with the must and the metal shavings on the floor made sense. She looked at his hands on the steering wheel, noticing how they rippled with pink scars, some fresh, some old.

"That's cool," Mia said. She'd only met a handful of welders in her life, one being a man she and Jack met in Taiwan. He was also an American on vacation, but he'd been visiting family. She remembered his hands were the same and that he wore sunglasses even inside.

"Does it hurt being a welder?" she asked.

He grinned, his white mustache picking up crookedly with his lip. "Sometimes. If you don't use the right equipment and take safety precautions, you're bound to end up with skin cancer and scars and even become blind."

Mia had no idea.

He took her silence as a chance to talk more. "But then again, most jobs don't give you enough time to take those precautions."

She nodded, her eyes glancing back to his hands as he looked at her from the side of his eye.

"Go ahead." He took his right hand off the wheel and extended it to her. "Touch it."

His large hand presented itself to her, where she examined it further. Curly, brown hairs twisted around on his knuckles and little cuts and splits in his skin speckled the top of his hand. There were round and straight scars and even one that snaked his middle finger. Little craters had formed by his thumb, and on his pinky knuckle there looked to be a fresh burn, the blister drained but still red.

Mia took her hand and gently rubbed her index finger over the scars, unsure how to feel. She didn't want to do it, but with as much as he'd done for her, she felt obliged.

"That's thirty years of welding right there." He shook his head, pulling his hand away. "Ah, I've worn those leather gloves, but some days your hands just don't want to work around them. You feel like you can't grip anything and like you're useless, so you strip 'em off and get to work."

Mia felt that was how she'd dealt with Jack. She had struggled with him long enough, losing her grip on reality until she finally let him go. Tears rose to the surface, but she pushed them down. She wouldn't cry for him again.

"What's your name, by the way?" he asked, retrieving her from her thoughts.

"*Oh*," she said, holding a hand to her mouth. "I can't believe I didn't introduce myself." A thought entered her mind.

Don't say your real name.

And in that instant, she said, "I'm Lisa."

"Lisa. Well, hi, Lisa. I'm Carl." He extended his hand, waiting for Mia to shake it.

She shook it, feeling the grooves under her fingers yet again.

"The parts store is only a few minutes away," he said, putting his hand back onto the steering wheel.

"Okay," Mia said.

The rest of the drive was quiet. Mia spent her time looking out the window between glances at Carl. He had to be in his fifties, with deep laugh lines around his eyes and mouth. His eyes were a striking blue, something that startled her when he stared too long, as if somebody had parked and left the headlights on in their car.

Or like a semi-truck coming head-on with you.

His nose was big, like bigger than Mia had most likely ever seen. The bridge of it pointed and plateaued and sloped down to the tip, and she realized she'd only seen this type of nose in cartoons. As she'd seen earlier, when he smiled, his two front teeth were large and slightly pointed outward, like they were trying to escape his mouth.

After smelling his cigarette filled breath, she couldn't blame them.

When they pulled up, the snow on the sidewalk in front of the store had to be six inches deep. Mia looked down at her sneakers, then over to Carl's warm-looking boots. She shook her head as she got out, damning herself for getting into this situation.

Carl opened the door for her, sounding a small bell, and said, "Don't worry, darlin', we'll be out of here soon."

They walked in under the eyes of three bored clerks. Mia watched them react to an older white man walking in with a younger Chinese woman, noticing how quickly they glanced away. Carl led her through the store to a wall of black boxes.

"These are the batteries, and I swear I remember a number on yours, but let me check the manual."

"Manual?"

"Yeah, there's a little book here." He picked up a fat, weathered book which hung from a chain on the wall. "If you know the make, model, and year of your car, we can figure out the battery."

Mia walked over and went through the list of car makers and models and years, finally pointing to a page number. "Page 349." She flipped through, quickly finding the page, and pointed to a string of letters and numbers.

"That'll be it." Carl walked over to the shelf and selected a battery while Mia let the manual go, the chain rattling as it caught the book. "You wanna hold it?" he asked.

Mia thought his face looked funny, like he was holding back a laugh. "Sure?" she said, extending her hand.

Carl handed over the battery, keeping one hand on the handle and one hand underneath. Mia took the handle, and when he let go, he held part of the weight with the hand under it. Mia jerked downward, a strange noise coming from her throat. Carl caught it before she fell and took it from her hands.

Putting a hand on her shoulder, he laughed and said, "Sorry, hon, I had to." He laughed again and walked away toward the register.

Mia stood there under the fluorescent lights, the smell of motor oil, air fresheners, and cleaners mingling in her nose as a fresh feeling of embarrassment reddened her face. She stood there until she realized she had to pay and scurried up next to him at the counter.

"That'll be a hundred dollars and thirty-three cents," the clerk, a large man with a spray of acne on his cheeks, said.

"A hundred dollars?" Mia asked.

Carl grinned. "Yeah, it's either that or you set up home in that motel you're parked at."

Mia sighed and handed over the money in cash. The clerk handed her the change back and she carefully tucked it into her wallet.

I need to start saving.

Carl picked up the battery and thanked the clerk. He gently put a hand on Mia's back, guiding her out of the store.

In the cab of his truck, Carl set the battery on the seat between them, and backing out of the space, he asked, "You got a man?"

Mia's eyes widened and her mouth hung agape slightly before she clamped it shut. Carl looked at her expectantly. "I—"

What do I tell him?

"I used to."

They left the parking lot, and he said, "I saw the little indent on your ring finger. You know, the spot where a ring might've used to be."

"Yeah." Mia crossed her arms across her chest, chewing on her lip. She averted her eyes from him, afraid if she made eye contact he'd see right through her; that he'd see who she was—how weak she was—and eat her whole.

"I got divorced once."

Without looking over, she said, "Yeah?"

"Yeah, she was a real bitch."

She looked over to see if he was smirking. He was not. She thought of the man in the gas station—the one who admitted to killing his wife with her own meds. Mia was sure it was the truth, as sure as she was sure Carl thought his wife was a bitch.

"You know," he looked over at her, "you look mighty familiar."

Mia's eyes widened. He took note of this.

"Not—" he cleared his throat, "not because you're Asian, you know."

Mia raised an eyebrow at him. "*I'm Chinese*," she said.

"Oh." Carl returned his gaze to the road. "How nice."

Mia and Carl sat in tense silence as he rolled down the road to the hotel. Patches of ice blotted the street, ready to make his tires slip. He cleared his throat once again but said nothing, and Mia kept her mouth tightly shut.

As soon as they parked, Mia got out of the cab and back into the freezing air. Her toes had the worst of it, her sneakers having soaked up icy water from in front of the parts store. Carl got out and brought the battery along with him. He asked her to pop the hood, and she obliged without a word.

Bent over into the engine compartment, Carl removed her battery with ease. Mia watched him carefully in case she'd ever have to do something like this alone.

It was dark. It was cold. And Mia was uncomfortable.

This man was traveling in the same direction as her. What if he were to follow her? He knew what she looked like, what she drove, and where she was headed. He could have her *just like that*.

She thought all this over as he finished up.

"Welp, that'll do it. Try startin' her up."

Again, she did so without a word, thankful the car started right up. She got out, a small smile on her lips. Carl stood, looking into the car with a grin of his own.

"Thank you," she said. She hated saying it, but it was necessary. He'd most likely saved her life.

"No problem, Miss Lisa." He gave her a wide grin. "What'll you be up to?"

"Oh." Mia thought for a moment, fiddling with her sweatshirt sleeves. "I'll probably be getting back out on the road." She nodded with an affirming smile.

"Out in this weather?"

"Yeah." She nodded faster and harder, thinking she probably looked like a lunatic.

"You oughta be careful, *Lisa*." He shook his head, closing her hood. Walking around to her side of the car, he stopped a foot from her, looking deep into her eyes.

Mia looked up, her heart racing.

He licked his lips and said, "Wouldn't want *anyone else* to have to rescue you."

The emphasis on *anyone else* made Mia nauseous. Her gut tensed up, and she clenched her jaw. "I—" she stopped, finding herself speechless.

"You be a good girl and get a room." He said it and walked away, then got into the cab of his truck.

Mia stood out in the cold as he started his truck and pulled away. Her nose ran, so she sniffled, the noise startling her. She glanced up at the hotel. The large building towered over her, its many windows like eyes glowing.

Well, it's hard to go mad at a hotel full of people, right?

No. No. I can't.

He left though.

Doesn't matter. I need to find another place to stay.

Oh, yeah, why don't you sleep in your car so you can freeze to death?

Oh, shut up.

She stomped her foot, stamping down fresh snow.

The clouds had cleared in the night, revealing a white, full moon. Mia looked up to it, wondering what Jack might be doing.

She climbed into her car, having left it running, and turned the heater on high.

I could have died today.

Stay here. Please, just sleep.

Mia shook her head and sighed, her shoulders slumping. She grabbed her purse and the night bag she had prepared for hotel stays and hopped out of the car. Locking it behind herself, she walked toward the mouth of the beastly building.

"*Hi, welcome to Motel Nine,*" a woman with big, blonde hair said from behind a counter. The lobby walls were a sponged yellow, and the room held a great, big hearth to the right side of the doorway, directly across from the desk. The desk itself was a dark wood, wrapped around the clerk in a large circle. Dark leather chairs and couches filled the rest of the waiting area, along with artwork from carved wood on the walls.

Mia approached the desk, her purse in hand. "I'd like to rent a room."

"Alright." The woman clicked around on her computer. "Just a small one or a suite?"

"It's just me, so a small room, please."

"Mmhmm. Looks like the only rooms we have right now are on the backside of the building."

"Backside of the building?"

"Yes, you access them from outside rather than coming in here."

"Oh." Mia thought about how far her car was and the snow.

"Yeah, not sure why they designed this building like that, but I can give you a discount on it." The clerk leaned forward, whispering, "No one has to know."

Mia nodded, leaning back away from the woman. "Yeah, uh, that'll work. Is there parking back there?"

"Yes! You can pull your car around. I'm sure that lot is empty right now. Not many people even realize there's rooms back there, especially with the storm and all."

Mia absently nodded, thinking the woman was much too chipper for a night like this.

"Your card, please?"

"Oh." Mia slipped one out of her wallet and handed it to the woman.

The woman looked at it, narrowing her eyes. "Uh, not to be one of *those people*, but you don't look like a *Jack*."

Mia took the card back, saying under her breath, *"Oh, shit."* She slid it back in and grabbed another card. "Here. This one is mine."

"Can I see your ID?" the woman asked, her genial tone having disappeared.

Mia rolled her eyes, fatigue making her irritable. "Ma'am, that's my husband's card."

"I don't see a ring."

Mia's eyes widened and her nostrils flared. *"You don't see a ring because I'm leaving his ass. Now let me pay for a room before I—"* she stopped, grabbing at the skin between her eyes and rubbing. "Just let me get a room without any trouble, please. I already crashed my car today. I don't need any more of this shit."

The clerk sat frozen in her seat, the gears clearly turning in her mind. Meanwhile, Mia stared at a spot of lipstick smeared above the woman's lip. Looking down at her neck, she noticed a small purple hickey.

The door behind the clerk opened, and a man walked in. He was at least ten years younger than the clerk and had a smudge of lipstick on his cheek. The clerk spun around, giving the man a small wave. He returned it with a smile, using his other hand to adjust the button on his uniform shirt. He appeared to be part of the cleaning staff.

The clerk pointed to her own cheek, and the man's eyes widened. He took the sleeve of his shirt and wiped away the lipstick, rushing into another room.

When the clerk spun around, Mia smirked and said, "You've got a little something on your neck." She pointed a finger at the hickey, barely poking the still frozen appendage from her sweatshirt.

The clerk's eyes widened, and she lifted her left hand to her neck, at the spot Mia was pointing at.

Mia noticed the giant rock on her finger. "Your husband get you that ring?" she asked.

The clerk remained frozen, but slowly nodded. Meanwhile, the young man came back from the storage room just off the lobby. He awkwardly smiled at Mia, unbeknownst to the other smudge of lipstick just next to his own lips.

Mia said, "I love that shade of lipstick."

The man threw a hand to his face and quickly wiped it off, his eyes darting around the room, avoiding Mia's sharp gaze.

Mia looked down at the clerk. "It looks just like yours." She tilted her head to the side, staring deep into her eyes.

"Here's your room, ma'am," the clerk said.

"Well, thanks," she said, taking her card back. "What room number?"

Averting her eyes back to the computer and moving the mouse around as if she was working, she said, "Two-fifty-two."

"*Thanks,*" Mia said, taking her bags and walking out of the lobby and back into the cold.

Back in her car, Mia hoped it would start. Carl acted like he knew so much, but what if it didn't work? What if something major was wrong?

What if I'm stranded in this shithole?

The car started without an issue, and Mia made her way to the back lot, looking up at the rooms. They spanned all the way up the huge building.

Getting out of her car and staring up at them, she wondered how many people had jumped to their deaths right where she stood.

Fucking dark.

The back of the motel was much like the back of anything, unseen and unkempt. Lights that barely lit the walkway flickered above her as she made her way up a flight of stairs. Upon arriving on the first floor, she realized it held more rooms than she expected. She'd have to go up a few more flights. Carrying her bags with her, she grunted more with each step. Her hot breath puffed out in clouds in front of her as the air froze the sweat on her forehead.

Burning off that Thanksgiving fat, dear.

Fuck off.

Halfway through the third flight, Mia heard footsteps behind her. She hastened her pace as much as her burning calves would allow, but they steadily approached. Her mind ran through every possible scenario.

A mugger aims his pistol in your face, asking you to hand over your wallet.

That man from the lobby runs up the stairs and punches me in the face, leaving me unconscious to freeze to death on these fucking stairs.

A man rushes up and pulls a knife, telling me to pull my pants down before—

"Excuse me."

Mia jumped. Spinning around, she dropped her night bag, balled her hand into a fist, and bared her teeth.

A small old woman stood on the landing below, her hands raised in submission and eyes wide in fear.

Mia instantly relaxed. "Oh, my goodness." She sighed, shaking her head and picking up her bag. "Yes?" she asked, trying to get herself to stop trembling.

"I was wondering if you could help me, but I've got it." The woman set to work trying to get up another stair. Her cheeks and nose were beet red, and her hand trembled as it reached for the handrail.

"No—" Mia set down her bags on the landing only a few steps ahead of her. "Here."

She walked down the stairs, extending her hand to the old woman.

The woman looked up to her, like a dog unsure of a stranger on the street.

Is she going to bite me?

"You're not going to punch me?" she said in the kindest way.

Mia laughed, taking the woman's cold hand. "No, I'm—I'm so sorry."

"Okay. It's not my first fight, but I'll be damned if it wouldn't be my last."

Mia helped her up the first step, then the second, and then the third, before the woman said anything else.

"I made it up those last two flights just fine, but, oh Lord, if my knees don't stop hurting, I might have to just lie down here for the night."

"I can't believe they don't have an elevator," Mia said.

"Oh, they do."

Mia snapped her eyes to the woman. "They do?"

"Oh, yeah," she rolled her eyes, "but it's broken."

"Oh, crap. Well, what's your room number?"

"Two-o-two."

"Ah, you're probably on the floor below mine. Only a half a flight and you should be there."

"Thank you."

At a snail's pace, the woman made it up the stairs with Mia holding her arms the entire time.

"I've got it from here, dear," she said on the landing.

"You sure?" The cold was getting to Mia. She couldn't feel the tips of her fingers anymore.

"Yes, thank you. Have a lovely night." The woman waved back at her without even a glance as she hobbled off.

Mia shrugged her shoulders, grabbed her bags, and began taking the next flight two steps at a time. The landing had a patch of ice from a leaky gutter she barely avoided. Peeking around a corner, she saw the balcony out front of the rooms was empty. Not a soul out, not even to smoke a late-night cigarette.

She rushed to her door, anxious to get inside and get warm. Fumbling with her key, she wondered, *What sort of place still uses keys?*

Anyone can copy a key.

A shiver ran up Mia's spine when she heard footsteps again.

She almost prayed to turn around and see the old woman.

Instead, Carl met her. A flash of panic spread through her body, and although she tried to keep it under wraps, Carl could see every one of her muscles contract.

He waggled a key in the air. "*Looks like we're neighbors,*" he said, smiling.

The lights on this flight were not white fluorescents, rather they were dim, yellowish bulbs in round glass housings, as if they hadn't been replaced since the seventies. This yellow light illuminated Carl's face in the most obscure way, leading the viewer to believe he didn't have half of his face and that the other half was sickly.

Mia nodded with a false smile and slipped her key into the door.

Please don't touch me. Please don't touch me. Please don't—

"I thought you were headed out for the night?" He stepped closer.

Mia chuckled, more out of nervousness than anything else. She looked at him from the corner of her eye, suddenly feeling safer out on the balcony than in the hotel room.

You're going to unlock that door, and he's going to shove you in and shut the door behind himself. He'll lock it and bind you up, gagging you so you can't scream. And then only God knows what's next.

She removed the key from the lock and stood to face him, giving the facade that she had confidence. "I got in my car and realized how tired I am," she said, her smile faltering slightly. She trembled, and she hoped he would think it was from the cold.

He warmly smiled and stepped away from her. "I get it." He unlocked his room's door and gave a wave. "Have a good night."

Mia repeated his words, adding *too* at the end, and watched the door close behind him.

She quickly turned to her door and stuck the key in the lock as quickly as possible. She cranked it over, listening to the deadbolt swing open. Then she stuck it in the handle and heard its faint *click*.

Mia barreled into the room, tossing her bags inside before swinging the door shut behind herself. She flicked over the locks before turning on a light. Spinning around with her back against the door, she could see the corner of the bed from the square of dim, yellow light casting from the window. She threw the small sashes closed, not giving a rat's ass about the view of the snowy landscape in the moonlight out ahead of her room.

In the darkness, she stood, panting, with her fingers still intertwined in the fabric of the window coverings. They were silky and cold, and—

Are they wet?

Mia pulled her hands back, smudging her fingers together. She didn't feel any wetness, but she could have sworn the curtains were damp. Sighing, she turned the light on.

A bedside lamp and a ceiling light in a white glass dome illuminated the room in a more cheerful glow than the lights outside provided. The bed sat up against the wall—the wall of which she shared with Carl. She shook her head and picked up her night bag, setting it on the red bedspread. A toothbrush was what she was after until she realized she might stink. She lifted the collar of her sweatshirt and stuck her nose in, inhaling.

Oh, yeah, we definitely need to shower.

A thumping came from behind Carl's wall, and Mia jumped. She thought about those movies where two people rented rooms beside each other, and one, unbeknownst to the other, would drill a hole in the wall they shared and watch them during their stay. With a shudder, she walked into the bathroom.

The entire room had a faint smell of must, most likely coming from mold behind one of the walls, but in the bathroom, it hit her like a loaded semi-truck. She covered her nose with her sleeve, wondering if it was even safe to breathe. The bathroom did not match the *ranch-style warmth* of the rest of the motel. Instead, it had pink floor and counter tile, and Mia had to ask herself if she hadn't accidentally walked into a ninety's grunge music video.

I know *there are lines of coke on this counter.*

She grinned behind the shirt sleeve and looked at the shower. Surprisingly, the motel had fitted the shower with a glass door. It was dirty, but one could see through it and that's all that Mia cared about. She stepped toward it, opened the door, and switched on the water. It came out in high pressure streams and quickly warmed, steaming up the glass.

Mia walked back into the bedroom, almost certain she would see Carl standing over the bed, his blue eyes blazing into her soul and a sick grin on his face. No one met her, but she felt unsafe all the same. She snatched up her night bag and checked the front door again.

Locked.

Locked.

As an extra precaution, she even slid over one of the chairs and wedged it under the door handle. It was a bit short, but she hoped it would at least alert her if someone was opening the door.

Her clothes bunched up in a pile on the pink tile, Mia stepped into the shower. She cursed herself for not bringing her flip-flops from the car, thinking of all the dirt and fluids that had drained down people's bodies and flowed over the floor into the drain. Her body tensed as she set foot in the shower, but the hot water hitting her shoulder helped her relax.

She started off by shampooing and conditioning her hair, and as she closed her eyes and leaned her head back, she worried someone might be there when she opened them.

Washing her body and face went quickly. She didn't feel the need to scour her skin like she did at home despite being in a shower hundreds—if not thousands—of people had cleaned themselves in before. With no sound accompanying her besides the running and splattering of water, Mia found herself enjoying the scent of her body wash and finally relaxing. Tears welled in her eyes, and she let herself cry, the dam having overflowed. She sobbed, her tears quickly washed away by the spray of water. They were loud, hysterical sobs that she could not control that made her sound like a wounded animal. Her face constricted, scrunching and twitching as she crouched down. The water gently hit the back of her head as she leaned her elbows on her bent knees and covered her face. Her nails dug into her forehead as she wailed. She spoke no words between these sobs, and she had no words to scream upward because there were none left to express how she felt.

Mia brought with her a clean sheet, which she spread out over the bed. She tucked the elastic corners as deep under the mattress as she could considering it was attached to the frame it sat on. Laying down on the sheet, the gentle scent of florals filled her breaths, rather than the musty smell of the bed. The layer of dust about the room indicated it hadn't been used in a long time, and Mia didn't plan on sleeping in an inch of fibers and skin cells.

Sleepily and with eyes half closed, she retrieved a blow-up pillow from her bag and set to work slowly filling it up. Had she thought about it, she would have ordered a small pump to avoid this. With each blow, she became more tired. The day had worn her down even worse than the last.

Looking over at the digital clock beside the bed, she saw it was 1:00 a.m.

I gotta start sleeping earlier, she thought.

She quickly closed the cap on the pillow and checked its firmness before setting it at the head of the bed. Getting up, she looked at each corner of the room and the bathroom doorway before flicking the lights off and scurrying into bed. In her pajamas, which were essentially the same as what she'd been driving in, she threw a blanket she'd brought with her over herself and curled into the fetal position. She held her hands close to her chest, trembling to generate heat. The heater feebly blew from the vent in the corner, puffing up dust and making a faint ticking sound.

Mia closed her eyes, which were still red from crying. The hum of the heater and the warmth her body was producing under the blanket quickly lulled her into the first stages of sleep.

Someone moaned.

Her eyes popped open, scanning the darkness around her. She remained frozen under her blanket, feeling its protectiveness around her.

And there it was again: a gentle, soft moan.

It sounded closer this time, yet muffled.

It's coming from next door.

She heard it again, this time even closer, then again, much closer in succession.

Each time she heard it, it grew louder. She shuddered with each one, feeling as if a stranger was doing it right in her ear. She knew good and well who it was.

Carl.

Yeah, Carl, on the other side of this wall, fucking himself.

He let out a louder moan, as if he heard her thoughts—as if he knew she was thinking of him.

Mia put a hand over her ear and under her head, squishing her palms into her ears, and yet, she still heard his moans. Louder and faster, they came until she heard him scream.

Silence.

Mia's mind gave her images of the mess he'd surely made on the wall right above her head. She thought how he would most likely leave it for the cleaning lady or next visitor to find. Her mind also wondered what he was going to do next.

Sleep?

God willing.

The heater's hum filled her mind, allowing her to close her eyes once more. She felt her body relax into the lumpy mattress as little thoughts blew around in her mind, all melding into chaotic images and scenes until they slowly didn't make sense anymore. They all faded to the back of her mind until her eyes snapped open.

Flesh.

Pink, wrinkled flesh took up her entire view. She gasped, and it moved aside, exposing Carl. He stood over her—nude—looking down at her with those piercing eyes that seemed to glow in the light from the window. Moonlight and the yellow lights outside seemed to mix on his body, exposing scars and pits on his chest. Harsh shadows gave his skin a grotesque texture.

Above her face hung his penis. It was larger than any she'd ever seen and bright pink, as if it'd just been set into boiling water.

Carl grinned and said, "*I call it my hammer.*"

Mia recoiled into the bed, scared to roll onto the other side. Carl swung it toward her, almost pointing at her face with it. She couldn't tell if he was hard or if the scarring had permanently deformed it. Twisting, deep scars traced up and down the shaft, and the head was porous with deep craters.

"*You wanna touch it?*" he asked, inching it closer to her face.

Mia screamed and sat up, her eyes frantically searching the dark, empty room.

I gotta get out of here.

Looking over, she saw the curtains were still closed, and she flew over to the wall, flicking on the lights as soon as her fingers found the switch. She grabbed her things on the nightstand and threw them into her bag, then ran into the bathroom and grabbed her dirty clothes and toiletries. She tossed them in and ripped the sheet off the bed. It barely fit in the duffle bag, and she decided to just carry the inflatable pillow. She tucked it under her arm, zipped up her night bag, flung it over her shoulder, and snatched up her purse. A knife sat glistening in the yellow light at the top of her purse, and she slipped it into her pocket.

Barely moving the curtains, she peeked her eye out, looking first left then right, toward Carl's room. Seeing no one, she unlocked the deadbolt, then the door handle and slowly pulled the door open. It creaked softly on its hinges. Cold air hit Mia in the face, helping her to wake up.

She slipped out of the room and closed the door, and once outside her room, she noticed Carl's curtains were open.

The flight of stairs' entryway was wide open, ready for her to step through, but if Carl saw her—

He'll pull me into his room and kill me with his dick.

She turned around, seeing only a wall at the end of the balcony.

How is that even safe? she wondered.

Turning around, she decided to go for it. Walking past his door, she crouched down and waddled under the window like a human duck, her duffle bag scraping the concrete.

Please don't see me. Please don't—

A door creaked open—*behind her.* She spun around to look, seeing nothing. Heart racing, she waited for a head to pop out of any of the doors behind her. She glanced over at Carl's, noticing it was still tightly shut. Images of the old woman poking her head out of a door filled her mind, and she remembered there were other people at the motel other than her and Carl.

She stood up on the other side of the window, looking back once, and made a run for the stairs. Never had she run downstairs so fast. Two at a time, she was down all four flights of stairs before she could finish *Camptown Races* in her head.

At her car, Mia looked up to the motel rooms, expecting to see Carl's head hanging over the balcony. Seeing nothing and no one, she threw her stuff into the car and got in. She started it, half expecting it to not start.

I bet Carl would do something like that.

He helped you, but he's a weirdo.

Yeah, duh.

She backed out of the spot and drove around front, parking in a vacant spot by the front door. The heater hadn't warmed yet, and Mia wondered if it ever would with how cold it was outside.

"Hi, how can I help you?" a different clerk said from behind the front desk. She had brunette hair to her ears in what Mia thought looked like a rancid bowl cut.

Mia cleared her throat, it having been irritated from crying only hours before. "I'd like to check out."

"Alright, I'll need your key and credit card."

Mia handed them over, and the clerk typed on the computer.

"Looks like you've only been here a few hours. What's got you leaving so soon?"

Mia had crossed her arms and was rubbing her elbows uncomfortably. "Just need to get back on the road."

The woman nodded and handed Mia her card back. "You have chains for your car?"

"Chains?"

"Yeah, so you can drive in the snow."

"You have to have chains to drive in the snow?" she asked, thinking *I really wish I wouldn't have taken ceramics.*

"Yeah, uh, it's even required in some areas. You don't have any in your car?"

"Does it look like I do?"

"Well—" the woman stopped, shrugging her shoulders. "I don't know. Most people here have them."

"I'm from California."

The woman's eyes widened. "*Oh.*" She laughed. "Yeah, there's no beaches or surfboards in this part of the country."

Mia narrowed her eyes, glancing over the woman's thick freckles before looking back to her eyes. "I'm from *Northern California.* I haven't been to a Californian beach in three years."

"Uh." The clerk looked back at the computer, chewing on her bottom lip nervously.

"Where can I get some chains?"

She looked back at Mia. "We actually sell them here."

"Of course you do. How much?"

"Fifty dollars and I'll install them free of charge."

"Deal."

Mia watched as the woman dawned thick gloves and went outside. She looked over Mia's car and measured her tires with a tape measure before running back inside. Returning, she brought with her snow chains.

"They're actual chains?" Mia asked. She'd expected something else despite the name.

"What—what else would they be?"

"I don't know." Mia turned away from the clerk, staring at the moon. "What's your name?" she asked, a snowflake landing on her nose.

"Al." She grunted, dropping a set of chains on the ground by the front driver's side tire.

"Is it short for anything?"

Al swept around the hood of Mia's car, setting the chains beside the passenger front tire. "Yeah," she paused, panting and puffing clouds out of her mouth, "Al."

Mia nodded, looking back at the woman. She walked around the car to watch as Al bent down and threw the set onto the tire.

She fiddled with it, getting it centered and straight before hooking some pieces together. Al stood with a grunt.

"Why do you do this?" Mia asked as Al made her way to the other side of the car.

"I've seen too many accidents out here."

Mia nodded.

"Now, get in and drive forward."

"Drive forward?"

"*Yes.*" She sighed. "I'll tell you when to stop."

Mia did so and got back out of the vehicle while Al fastened the chains the rest of the way on and switched sides. "All done," she said.

"Thank you so much. I—I may or may not have gone off the road earlier."

"Oh, yeah?"

"Yeah, luckily this guy came and helped me."

The color drained from Al's face and, with wide eyes, she looked from the car to Mia. "What did he look like?"

Mia shrugged her shoulders. "Uh—like an older guy. Patchy, white hair. *Oh,* and these crazy blue eyes."

Al backed away from Mia with a step. "Where did he go?"

Mia looked at Al questioningly. "He took me here—"

"*Here?*"

"Yeah, then to the parts store for a battery, and then back here."

"Did you get any weird feelings about him?"

Mia nodded. "Oh, yeah, big time. Why do you think I'm leaving?"

Al stepped back toward Mia, anticipation on her face. "Why?"

"He ended up getting the room next to mine."

"*Are you serious?*" Al's entire body tensed.

"*Yes. Why?*"

She peered around Mia and got close to her face, puffing steam between them. Shaking, she put her lips to Mia's ear and whispered, "*He tried to kidnap me… I think he's a serial killer.*"

Mia drove on the freeway slowly, the chains freaking her out. Her lower lip was bleeding. She could taste the tangy blood, yet she continued to gnaw at it.

The snow came down in gentle snowflakes, only a few at a time, but Mia didn't see them. She barely saw the road. Her mind was encapsulated by *Carl*.

Carl the serial killer.

Images flashed in her head of every detail about the man, even the ones that weren't real, and she drove in the direction she hoped would bring her home.

Chapter Nine: Scrambled Eggs and Blood

Please, just let me drink something sweet. Something! Anything! I'll even take hot tea with a spoonful of sugar. Dear God, I feel like shit.

Jack opened his eyes, his tongue writhing in his mouth, dry as the desert. The sun had risen high into the sky, sending blinding light through the white curtains of his bedroom.

"*Deryk?!*" he yelled.

A few minutes passed before Rochelle popped her head in. "What's up, dear?"

"Where's Deryk?"

Rochelle walked up to the bed, shutting off Jack's CPAP and carefully taking his mask off. "I called him and told him not to come in until this afternoon."

"*Why?*"

"Well, I figured you would want to sleep in." She smiled, touching his arm.

Jack pulled it away. "I'm supposed to be getting up early."

"For what?"

"*For my morning exercise videos.*"

Rochelle laughed, waving him off. "Jack, you know no one is watching those."

"*There are people watching them,*" he hissed.

Rochelle shrugged. In a baby voice, she said, "You just looked so tired laying there. I just wanted to let you rest."

The front door opened, changing the pressure in the room briefly.

"I'm here!" Deryk yelled from downstairs.

Rochelle looked at the doorway with a glare. "*Well, isn't he early?*" She scooted out of the room, calling to Jack, "I'll be back in a minute!"

"*Deryk! Deryk!*" Jack cried. "*Please help me out of bed!*"

Deryk raced up the stairs, stopping as Rochelle stood in front of him.

"*Move,*" he said, looking into her eyes.

Rochelle stared back, her jaw set. "*You* will stay *out of the way* as *I* help him out of bed."

Deryk raised his palms up in surrender. "Hey, it's your back."

He followed Rochelle up the staircase, wondering how he was going to pry Jack's body off of her.

Jack saw Rochelle walk into the room first and, at that moment, wished he hadn't invited her to his home.

You didn't invite her. She invited herself.

"Come on, Jackie. I'll help you out of bed." Rochelle held her hands out to him, and he slapped them away.

"Stop fucking around, Rochelle. I'm like three times your size." He sighed. "Deryk, can you help me please?"

Deryk nodded and stepped forward, pushing Rochelle aside. She left the room, pouting.

"Why is she in one of your shirts, Jack?" He smirked, pulling down the handle Jack used. "Don't tell me y'all did the nasty last night."

Jack laughed, and Rochelle cringed as she descended the staircase. She silently mocked his buttery laughter as she slammed down onto the couch and turned on the TV that hadn't been on in years.

"No, we didn't. We just talked about life."

"About your life with Mia?" Deryk asked, sliding a gait belt around Jack's waist. "Lean forward," he said.

Jack shook his head and leaned forward. "No, no. Mainly about what we want out of life. Who we are—"

"Jack," Deryk paused for a grunt as he fastened the belt, "do you even *know* who you are?"

"Well, sure I do. I'm Jack Butchere. I like to make videos. I like to make people smile—"

"*And cum to your food videos,*" Deryk said. He laughed and gripped the handles of the gait belt. "Up," he commanded, like a trainer to a dog.

Jack stood up and balanced with one hand on the handles, which hung from the ceiling, and one hand out like a ballerina. He wobbled like he was standing on a tightrope. Deryk steadied him by gripping his elbows, and Jack made eye contact with him. "*I didn't know people had—had—*" he searched for the words, his eyebrows furrowing, "*Kinks! I didn't know people had kinks for that shit.*"

Rochelle heard *Kinks!* and quickly cocked her ear, turning the TV's volume down.

Jack laughed again, almost falling over. "I had no idea! It wasn't until someone commented on my video, one of the earlier mukbangs, and told me to search up this video."

"What was it?" Deryk asked, mesmerized. He let go of the gait belt, keeping his arms out as Jack tottered.

"I'm not telling you the phrase he told me to look up." Jack shook his head. "It was *rancid.*"

Deryk thought, *much like most of your videos.*

"But it involved a woman, a man, and a watermelon."

"A watermelon?" Deryk asked.

"Yes." Jack's eyes widened. "Don't. Look. It. Up."

Deryk laughed and assured Jack he wouldn't as he gripped the belt and lowered him in his chair. Jack had done well standing, and he thought for a minute before asking, "How would you like to go downstairs?"

Jack perked up like a dog who heard *walk*. "Downstairs?"

Deryk nodded, "Yeah, so you can see the kitchen and watch TV on something that is bigger than eighteen inches."

Jack looked down at himself, his cast, his chair, and then back to Deryk. "*How?*"

Images of the wallpaper rotating over and over flashed through Jack's mind. The pain was still fresh in his sides.

"*Buddy*, you've been training those knees—"

Rochelle broke in. "Downstairs?" she asked.

Deryk snapped a look at her, saying with his eyes, *Can you fucking not?*

"*Listen*," Jack said. "Deryk is the expert here. Let's listen to him."

With a smirk, Deryk said, "Well, with Rochelle here, it's even better because she can help. You've been building strength in your legs for days and just the other night you stood on your own!"

Jack nodded, very clearly proud of himself.

"Has he even walked?" Rochelle asked.

"Not much, but he's about to." Deryk held out a hand to Jack. "You got this."

With Deryk's words, Jack suddenly felt light, like he'd instantly shed two-hundred pounds. Deryk pulled on the belt as Jack pushed himself from the chair. The hardwood creaked under his weight, but there he stood on one foot.

"Rochelle, move the chair out of the way and grab that crutch in the corner."

Rochelle hopped onto the chair and moved the lever, scooting it out of the way. Deryk rolled his eyes, knowing damn well she didn't have to get on the thing to move it. She ran to the crutch and handed it to Jack.

Deryk focused his attention back on Jack. Nervously, Jack clambered for Deryk's hand. Letting go of the belt, Deryk clasped his hand in Jack's and looked into his eyes. Jack stared back, reassured.

Jack forced his core to harden as much as he could get it to and put all his attention on standing up without Deryk. He tried to let go of his hand, forcing weight onto the crutch under his armpit.

Deryk shook his head frantically, clamping down on Jack's hand. "No, no. One thing at a time. *Holding onto me*, try lifting your good leg."

Jack took a deep breath and lifted his uncast foot, bending it at the knee.

"Good, now set it down and pick up the other."

Jack slowly lowered his foot and picked up the cast leg.

"That's great. Now steady yourself."

Jack closed his eyes and imagined he was a spinning top. His legs were the little point at the bottom that helped keep the top spinning, and the wider middle part was his body. He imagined how difficult it would be to balance a spinning top on its sharp point, and shifted the image so the top had great, big feet. The little point sat above the ground a few inches, in between a pair of ankles which connected to feet that would be impossible not to balance on. They were as wide as the top itself and so long as those little ankles could support it, the top remained balanced.

And like that, Deryk was no longer holding his hand or the belt. Jack was standing on his own, his one free hand out like a zombie. He smiled.

Deryk said in a tone so quiet that Jack had to strain to hear, "Now lift your foot."

Jack picked up his foot and didn't wobble. He set it down and picked up the other, not wavering.

"Now pick it up and set it a few inches in front of the other. Not too big of a step."

Jack concentrated on this, while in the back of his mind he thought of how much Deryk sounded like a nighttime radio DJ. The kind that played soft jazz and spoke softly.

There it was, his left foot a few inches from his right foot.

"Transfer the weight."

Jack leaned forward, pushing with his right foot and building pressure on his left. The weight transferred, and he stood a few inches away from where he'd been standing originally.

Deryk lifted his arms up and shook his fists, and Jack did the same, keeping his balance the whole time. His cast foot only ached a bit, but the pain was the furthest thing from his mind at the moment. He smiled broadly.

Rochelle watched, wishing she could be a part of this moment. She cheered a little, giving a halfhearted *woo* that no one noticed.

Why can't you help him like that?

He clearly likes Deryk more than you, and just a few days ago he was talking about eating you out.

Rochelle was mad. She was mad at herself, mad at Jack, but most of all, she was mad at *Deryk*.

She wished Jack would fall and hurt himself, finally realizing that Deryk was no good for him. Or better yet, she wished Jack would fall and crush Deryk, killing him without her having to lift a finger.

When Jack actually fell, she didn't expect it to be so loud.

He had stayed balanced through his victory, and when he felt unstable, he reached out to Deryk. Deryk took his hands as Jack dropped his crutch. He assumed Jack would fall toward him. Jack's knees gave out, buckling under his weight and sending him backward.

Deryk did the only thing he could think of: *he let go.*

And before Jack could fully fall, Deryk grabbed his ankles and yanked, hoping for the best. Jack landed on his back, wheezing and gasping. The entire floor shook, and the sound his bare back made hitting the wood flooring was like that of a shotgun.

Immediately, a wailing sound like that of a newborn escaped his mouth.

Deryk knew he would be in pain, if not broken, but he was glad Jack's knees hadn't been blown out.

"Are you okay?" Rochelle ran to his side, lifting his sweaty, bald head in her hand and setting it on her thigh as she sat on her knees beside him. He nodded, pouting, and Deryk left the room.

She didn't think it could have gone better—if only Deryk would slip on the stairs and smack his head. He'd abandoned Jack at such a time, *and* it was an event that was Deryk's fault.

Rochelle shook her head and caressed Jack's arm. He sniveled and cried but remained without words.

Deryk ran into the room less than a minute later with a bag in hand. He set it on the floor and rummaged through it, finally finding liquid pain medicine.

"You want some pain meds, buddy?"

Jack looked at Deryk, in a way that Rochelle wished he would look at her, and shook his head.

"No, I'm okay."

Deryk cocked his head to the side, surprised. "You sure?"

"Yeah." Jack began to cry harder. "*I'm just so ashamed of myself!*" he wailed.

Rochelle's heart broke a little, and Deryk knelt at his side. Before she could think of anything to say, Deryk was already speaking.

"Don't worry about it, man. We'll get through this."

"How—how am I going to get up?"

Rochelle realized that Jack didn't see Deryk at fault here. In fact, he seemed to be looking to Deryk for guidance.

Guidance through a situation that is clearly Deryk's fault.

"We'll pull your hoists down and get you up. You think you can sit up?"

Jack took a deep breath and nodded, taking Deryk's extended hand. Rochelle was pushed aside yet again.

Deryk pulled as Jack did the hardest crunch of his life.

Mia drove with both hands on the steering wheel. Her eyes and head hurt, and the noise from the chains on her tires was going to drive her mad. Signs passed her by slowly, but she didn't read them. She knew she needed to stay on the highway to get home.

Home.

She thought about sleeping on the couch in her own living room because her bed was too small to fit both her and Jack. She thought of the sickly damp smell that hung in the air in the house and the way sweat clung to her skin at all times. Most days it was Jack's sweat which wetted her body.

Driving a frozen car twenty-five miles per hour on a snow-covered freeway with no other cars in sight and a serial killer on the loose nearby, she'd do anything to sleep on that couch again.

Trying to shoo the thoughts away, she grabbed her phone. She opened her mom's chat, hit the call button, and waited. This time, she was quickly interrupted.

Your call has been forwarded—

She hung up, throwing her phone into the passenger side and sobbing. She'd left tens of messages already, and now the phone was off?

There was an exit up ahead that she could barely see.

Decision Road, the sign read.

I can't believe this corny shit.

Mia turned on her blinker for no one besides herself and got off on the exit. She was sent down a gravel road and quickly parked on the side of it, where she cried into her hands.

The snow began to fall, alongside her tears, and she was left with nothing but cold and regret.

Lying in bed ten minutes after his fall, Jack caught his breath. Rochelle and Deryk had left the room, as they'd agreed on the importance of brunch. He snatched up the TV remote and turned on the same cartoon he always watched. Meanwhile, Rochelle sat at the kitchen counter, pestering Deryk.

"So, you're really not going to let me have any?"

"No."

Rochelle hmmphed. "Can I have any leftovers?"

"*No,*" Deryk said, scrambling eggs with bell peppers, sausage, and cheese.

"*But it smells so good,*" she whined.

Deryk whipped around to look at her. "*How old are you?*"

Rochelle stiffened in her seat. "*Old enough to know you're an asshole.*"

Deryk rolled his eyes, hardly the reaction Rochelle wanted. He turned back to cooking and said over his shoulder, "Good luck surviving on ramen and TV dinners."

Rochelle grunted and got up out of the chair, determined to prove she could cook more than that, despite knowing she couldn't. She first looked in the fridge, then the pantry, then the fridge again. Both were entirely stocked, but she didn't know what to choose.

Deryk had taken over most of the kitchen, leaving her with the microwave and air fryer at the end of the counter. She grabbed a box of frozen lumpia and read the instructions.

Deryk looked back at her and chuckled.

She gave him a dirty look right as he went back to stirring the eggs. They were bright and fluffy and chocked full of good food, and Rochelle found herself angry again. She opened the box of lumpia and dumped it out, the little rolls falling out in a plastic bag. Stomping over, she selected a knife from the knife block to open the plastic with. She looked it over, letting the bright lights above her glint off of it.

"You know, I'd thought you were a kindhearted soul having feelings for Jack, but now I see you're just a greedy little piggy, just like hi—"

The knife jutted from Deryk's Adam's apple. His eyes widened and he clawed at the back of his neck, reaching for the handle. In all his years of working as a nurse, he'd never seen the worst of the worst. The things he saw were a walk in a meadow compared to things ER doctors and paramedics saw. *And now he'd become another story they'd tell their friends.*

He choked and grabbed the handle of the knife, unsure whether he should rip it out or keep it in. Blood pooled in his lungs and sprayed out onto the stovetop and eggs with every cough. He figured he must've been lucky she missed his brain stem, but also wondered if that instant death would have been better.

Deryk was amazed at how calm he was despite his body's spastic movements. He turned around to see Rochelle smiling and leaning against the fridge. Her arms were comfortably crossed across her chest as if she were posing for a casual photo.

Drowning in his own blood, Deryk reared back his hand and swung down, smacking Rochelle across the face. He struck her hard enough to knock her down, effectively causing him to lose his balance. His shoe slipped in his blood, and he fell flat on his stomach on the linoleum.

Rochelle got up on her hands and knees, holding her reddened cheek. Deryk convulsed on the floor, the knife having been pushed partially out of his throat from the fall. Blood pooled around him, the puddle growing larger by the second.

Rochelle stood up and dropped a knee onto his back. She snatched the knife with her right hand, sure to twist it to tear up more flesh on the way out, and grabbed his hair with her left hand. Deryk screamed, gargling blood. Lifting his head up, Rochelle took the knife and aimed it under his left ear. In one sweep, she slit his throat open from ear to ear.

Deryk garbled and suction noises came from where his windpipe was exposed. Blood sprayed before him like a waterworks show, and Rochelle shrieked with victory.

She threw the knife down and smashed Deryk's face into the floor as one last *fuck you* before standing up. Looking down at his body, she appraised his weight and height, pleased that a girl so much smaller could do such damage. Turning away from him, she looked at the stove. The eggs were about to burn, so she rushed over to turn down the burner and stir them.

"*Rochelle?!*" Jack called from his bed. He'd paused the TV and held his blanket to his chest in fear. "*Rochelle, are you okay?*" He trembled, waiting for someone with a machete to enter his doorway and chop him up.

"Yeah! I'm okay!" Rochelle called.

Jack's trembling did not go away.

If she's okay…

"*Deryk?! Deryk?! Are you okay?!*"

Rochelle took a fork that had been laid out for Jack and stabbed a hunk of egg and sausage out of the pan. Splatters of blood reddened the eggs to a strange orange color, and as Rochelle took a bite and chewed, she marveled at how the blood added much flavor.

I can't go back. I can't go back. I can't go ba—

160

Mia flipped around to leave *Decision Road*, and once she reached the exit, she didn't turn to go east. Instead, she crossed traffic—of which there was none—and turned to head west.

There's nowhere else that I feel needed.

She'd done all her crying in the car and had no tears left.

She's ignoring you.

She's not ignoring me. She could be in trouble. She most likely is *in trouble, but I'll go home. I'll book a flight after I check on Jack, and I'll be okay.*

We'll be okay.

Mia drove fifteen miles an hour before slowing down to ten. The road was slick, and she could feel it in the steering wheel. Her arms trembled, with exhaustion or exertion she did not know.

A few minutes passed as the road crept under her bumper, the front end of her car like a ginormous monster consuming the asphalt. Mia shook her head, trying to shake free the stupid thoughts. All they were doing was providing an escape for what she really wanted to think about.

"Go to California with him. He's a good man," her mother had said.

"We trust you to make the right decision. We'll be okay here," her father had told her.

And then COVID, fucking COVID. Fucking racist fucks couldn't just order takeout and shut up. Had to throw bricks and call my parents—

Is that—

Headlights?

Headlights appeared before her, swerving back and forth in both lanes ahead before centering in her lane. She slammed on the brakes, unsure what else to do, but even with snow chains on, her car continued forward. Mia screamed.

Her car glided freely as the headlights steadily approached, and without thinking, she stomped on the gas. The chains whipped wildly around her tires, and Mia's steering wheel ripped itself from her hands. She clumsily reached to bring it back to the center, her toes still forcing the accelerator down, when a wall of snow presented itself in her windshield. She screamed louder, the front end of her car coming into contact with the icy wall. What was once forgiving snow had hardened into ice, setting Mia's airbag off. It slammed into her chest with a heat that penetrated through her sweatshirt and left her gasping for air.

Black encircled her vision and floated in front of her in little wisps. She closed her eyes, her head leaning against the inflated airbag.

Warm. It's so warm.

Her car sputtered off, shutting down completely.

Minutes passed before headlights shone through her passenger window. The truck parked and out came a man. He ran to Mia's door, somehow not slipping on the icy road, and tugged her door open.

Mia opened her eyes.

"Carl?"

"Yeah."

She extended a limp hand. "How—"

"I was driving from the motel and saw you spin out...again."

"What luck." She closed her eyes again.

"Grab your phone, Mia."

She turned her head and looked at her phone in the passenger floorboard, then turned to look at Carl again. "It's so far though. So...far away." Her eyes closed again, and Carl heard her breathing even out.

He scooped her out of her seat and carried her through the heavy falling snow. "I gotcha, darlin'."

Setting her in the passenger side of his truck and buckling her in, he figured he ought to grab some of her things. He trudged back to her car and grabbed the keys, her phone, her night bag, and a bundle of clothes he saw on the back seat.

This girl was headed somewhere for good.

He shook his head, slamming the car door shut and locking it. He was surprised to hear it chirp but doubted it would be here longer than two days.

Back in the cab of his truck, he arranged her things between them and shook Mia's shoulder. "Where are we headed, dear?"

Eyes still closed, Mia's lips parted. Her hand went to her head, and she rubbed her temple. After a deep breath, she said, "California."

"Back to old Cali?" he asked.

"Yeah."

"Why?" He flipped the switch from hot air to cold air and turned the blower up.

When the cold air hit her on the cheek, Mia's eyes popped open.

Carl thought they looked to be dilating alright, and he hoped she didn't have a concussion. "Why are you headed back to California, Lisa?" he asked, slowly.

"I—" Mia shook her head. "My name is Mia."

"Oh," Carl smiled. "I done knew that."

"You did?"

"Hell yes, I did. Y'all were all my wife could ever talk about. *Mia and Jack did this, why can't we do that? Let's go to the Bahamas. Screw your job.*" He closed his mouth abruptly. "I'm rambling. Anyway, she thought y'all were the shining beacon of a healthy relationship, something she didn't think we were."

"I'm sorry."

"No, it's okay. I know y'all aren't perfect, but she was so blind. She left to the Bahamas one summer and never came back."

Mia chewed on her lower lip.

"*So*, why are you headed back?"

"I'm worried about Jack. I don't think he's well."

"You leave him in that chair all by his lonesome?"

"No, I left him with a nurse, but—" she paused, "I've got this wretched feeling."

"Yeah, well, I'll get you back there."

"All the way to California?"

"Sure, why not?" he said, leaving the side of the road.

Mia did not remember the headlights. All she could recall was spinning out of control and slamming into the snow.

Rochelle walked along the old, abandoned mining road, the gravel crunching underfoot. Deryk's car sat between some trees off the beaten path, a place she hoped it wouldn't be discovered for a few days. As she walked, heat prickled between her thighs.

A whole dead body and *my crush—a match made in heaven.*

She strolled along until she reached the asphalted road, where she flipped up the hood of Deryk's jacket and stuffed her hands in her pockets. She kept her head down, her face still spattered with blood.

Rochelle had only ever dreamed of being a killer. With every inconvenience in her life, she'd thought murder was the solution. When her neighbor's dog shit on her grass every day as a teenager, she daydreamed of slitting the dog's throat and bludgeoning the owner with its body. When a group of girls bullied her in high school, she began looking at her father's guns differently, wondering how it would feel to bring one to school and blow their brains out. Never in a million years did she think she'd get to live out her fantasies.

I'm going to carve Deryk's body like a delicate ham and serve it to Jack like the greedy pig he is.

Meanwhile, Jack cried in his bed. He could smell the burnt eggs and was almost certain he could smell the tangy, metallic scent of blood. His phone was nowhere to be found, and sure he was next, Jack had soiled himself. He lay in a puddle of piss, sweat, diarrhea, and tears, trembling.

The stairs in the hallway kept popping up in his mind. Even if he were able to get out of bed, he would *never* conquer the stairs without injuring himself.

Or breaking every bone in my body and bleeding out at the bottom.

He sobbed into his hands as Rochelle steadily approached on the road. Jack didn't realize how far she was, but he could feel in his heart just how far away Mia was.

The snow had fallen heavily, causing Carl to get off the freeway at a leisurely fifteen miles an hour. He drove over to a small motel, much quainter than the last one.

"This is the *Buena Casa*, and it's very expensive," he said.

Mia shook her head. "I have cash, but I'm trying to save."

"Well, let's see what the room'll cost," he said, parking.

They walked in together, Mia with her bag and a headache the size of Massachusetts. The lobby screamed 90s cottage house aesthetic, rather than the rugged and rough motel lobby she'd been in hours before. Even the woman at the counter looked like a relic of the 90s, of the *older* generation of course.

When the clerk said three-hundred dollars per night, Mia laughed. The clerk looked at her sternly through much-too-long bangs. Mia snapped her mouth shut.

"Really?" Carl asked.

"Really." She crossed her arms across her chest, her gleaming name tag reading *Sarah*.

Carl whipped out his wallet and handed the woman a fat wad of twenties. "Should cover it," he said gruffly. "Give me a room with heating, a nice shower, and a good view in this *shit* weather."

"I'll see what I can do," she said, her false smile saying *yeah-you'll-get-what-you-get*.

Room twenty-three would be their home for the night, and as she and Carl strode down the hallway—the hallway which was covered in blue carpeting with flowers and wallpaper with clouds on it—she felt the first pang of anxiety. The way the color had drained from that woman's face when she heard Carl was staying in the motel kept replaying in her mind. He was a creep, but she wasn't sure he was a killer.

He walked ahead of her, her night bag in his right hand. Carl limped in a way she hadn't noticed before, just a slight deviation from a normal step with his left foot. It swung out far as if he was avoiding something between his legs.

Carl glanced back at her and noticed her eyes were on his left foot. He'd thought he wasn't walking so strangely, but her gaze proved him wrong. Turning his head around just in time to avoid a bellhop, he said, "Damn cold makes my hips hurt."

Mia couldn't believe he knew she was staring. She nodded instead of saying anything before they ascended a flight of stairs.

Carl wheezed in front of her, really swinging his foot to get it up each stair. Mia offered to take the bag, but Carl pulled away with a grunt.

The second floor looked identical to the first. Maroon doors in a sky-blue hallway was not an ideal color choice in Mia's opinion. The repetitiveness of hotels had always given her the ick. How easily one could get lost down these identical corridors, especially someone without the ability to read numbers—like a child. A hotel like this might be easy to get out of, but those large, corporate hotels would be impossible without a map, she thought.

And here I am with a potential serial killer.

"Here we are!" Carl said, his smile wrinkling up his face. Room twenty-three sat in the middle of the second floor, between and across from rooms that appeared full. Signs like *do not disturb* and *out for a bite* hung from the doorknobs.

There will be someone to hear my screams.

He opened the door and a blast of heat hit them. Carl chuckled and said, "Guess the heater works," before stepping inside. Mia stood at the doorway, her feet rooting her in place.

One room. One bed. One serial killer.

Carl set down her bag on the bed and went off to explore the rest of the room. Mia watched him enter the bathroom before coming in. She set to work getting the bed covered before thinking about asking.

"Carl? Do you want the bed or the couch?"

He peeked his head out from the bathroom and saw her covering the bed.

"I-"

"Don't worry, I'll sleep on the couch." He smiled and retreated into the bathroom.

She felt guilty and almost prepared the couch for herself when she thought of how mad he might get.

I've been sleeping on a couch for how long now? I deserve *a bed.*

Okay, calm down. We're dealing with a possibly volatile man here.

So, Mia covered the bed with her fitted sheet, set up her pillow, and laid out a blanket for herself. Looking over at the couch, she thought she could spruce it up a bit. Taking the comforter from the bed, she folded it and draped it over the scratched pleather cushions. She set out the pillows from the bed on both couch arms, unsure which way he was going to lie, and, as a final touch, she found a blanket in the closet that she left folded on the seat.

Ruffling through her bag in search of her night guard, Carl came out of the bathroom in the same clothes and damp skin. He smiled.

"Oh, you didn't have to do all that, Mia." He walked over to the couch and ran his fingers across the comforter, which she'd laid soft side up.

"It's no big deal," she said, now frantically searching. She stopped and looked over at him. He sat on the couch, his hands on his knees, grinning. "I would have given you the bed if you just said so."

"Nah." He held his hand up and waved off the bed. "I usually sleep in the cab of my truck, so this is like the King's palace right here."

Mia smiled. "And I usually sleep on the couch." She chuckled.

"*You?*" Carl asked, standing up abruptly.

Mia flinched. "Yes."

"That man makes *you* sleep on the couch?"

She shrugged. "Well, he can't get downstairs."

Carl scoffed. "You ought to get him a pile of hay!" He shook his head and sat down.

Mia laughed. The image of Jack rolling around on a bed of hay tickled something in her brain. She thought of him munching on a piece of hay and lost it. She cackled, bending over with her hands on her knees.

Carl watched as her face turned red and tears crept from her eyelids. Sounding like a mule, she laughed, thoughts of Jack with a saddle on his back dancing in her head. She slapped her leg, trying to stop.

"You okay?" Carl asked, furrowing his brow.

She nodded, her laughs silent. Mia lost her balance, slipping onto her butt next to the bed. Carl nervously chuckled, his eyes glued to Mia as she covered her face with her hands and harshly breathed into them. She dug her fingernails into her face and took a deep breath. When she surfaced from her hands, her face and eyes glowed red. Carl blinked, and Mia was back on the bed.

She sighed. "I haven't laughed that hard in a *long* time."

Carl stared at her, uncomfortable. "Yeah?"

She took another deep breath and let it out. "Yeah."

Carl shook his head. "Well, I'm glad you got it out."

Mia chuckled and whinnied like a horse. Carl jumped, thinking the people in the room next to theirs must think they're insane.

"Oh, God, I could just see him growing his hair into a mane and eating hay on camera like he's some stud." She laughed softly, and shook her head.

Mia felt very suddenly empty, like every internal organ in her body had been removed, including her brain. TV static filled her insides as if she were between channels, and the smile on her face slowly faded.

Carl watched her, wondering how sane this girl was. "You okay?" he asked.

She looked at him, her eyes empty, and nodded. "Yeah."

The lights flickered, startling the pair, and before they could speak, the lights fully went out. The heater ceased its humming and the noise from the TV next door halted. Carl and Mia were left staring at each other in silence and the dim, gray light from the window.

"Honey, I'm home!"

Jack sat up, trembling in bed, as Rochelle pushed the sliding glass door open and slipped in. She left behind tacky blood on the white handle.

"*Honey?*" she called, taking in the smells of the house.

Jack stared at the dark TV screen before him, barely able to see his own reflection. His mouth opened, but no sound came forth.

I have nowhere to go.

He heard her footsteps quickly shuffle up the stairs.

"*Jaaaack,*" she whispered from just outside his door.

Silence.

Jack waited, facing the TV but looking out of the corner of his eye at the open doorway.

"*Jackie!*" She hopped into view, stamping her feet on the ground.

A short scream escaped him before he snapped his lips shut. Wide eyed, he stared at Rochelle as she approached him. The smile on her lips had spread to her cheekbones.

"*Jack*, you haven't even had your brunch yet, have you?"

Jack shook his head.

"I'll whip something up for you," she said, quickly spinning around and leaving the room.

Jack fidgeted with his fingers in his lap when a sickening thought struck him.

Oh my God, she's going to cook Deryk.

Much to his surprise, Rochelle came back with scrambled eggs and burnt toast. She presented it with her manic smile and watched him with a gleam in her eye. Jack took the plate and fork, looking at the eggs. The fork trembled in his hand as he poked at the scrambled chunks. He glanced up at Rochelle.

"Where's—"

"Don't worry about it."

He stared at her, anger rising in his chest. Opening his mouth to speak, Rochelle cut him off.

"I said, '*don't worry about it.*'" She chuckled, as if she didn't sound entirely deranged, and said, "Now eat your *eggs.*"

Jack doubted it was only eggs and toast on his plate, but with Rochelle smiling with her hands behind her back, he figured it was a better situation than being *on* the plate.

He scooped up a good mouthful of egg and slowly brought it to his lips. They smelled like eggs, but when he took a bite, he internalized a gag.

"What's the matter?" Rochelle asked, catching the way his mouth turned down.

Jack's eyes snapped up to her, the fork still in his mouth. He slid it out, the metal scraping on his teeth, and gave a sheepish grin. "Ah, they're just a bit cold."

Rochelle's smile slowly faded, and her voice became deep as she said, "*Eat it anyway.*"

Jack's eyes fell back to the plate, and he vehemently nodded.

By the time he finished the cold, scrambled eggs, the sun had almost fully set, leaving them in an almost pitch-black room. Rochelle's smile had returned. It glinted in the dim light.

She took his plate downstairs without turning on a light, leaving Jack in the dark. Slowly, the doorframe became less and less visible, and he prayed that he would at least hear her coming. With his heart heavy in his ears, he strained to listen.

"*Jack,*" she whispered, her breath tickling his ear.

He let out another short scream before her hand clamped over his mouth.

"I think it's bedtime, Jack."

Mia and Carl stared at each other for some time, each having questions about the other on the tips of their tongues. Neither said a thing until Mia asked if he was tired. He nodded, and off they went to sleep, Carl on the couch, Mia on the bed.

It took Mia a while to fall asleep. She listened to Carl breathe. Without the hum of the heater—or anything with power in the hotel—their breathing and shuffling was the only noise in the room. Carl's breaths slowly evened out and became gentle snores, and as Mia drifted off to sleep, she realized she couldn't remember what Jack sounded like when he slept without a CPAP machine.

In her dreams, she was back with her parents, having tea with her mother. She could taste the sweet tea and feel the sunshine on her skin. Birds chirped, her mother softly spoke, something about the restaurant, and Mia felt the grass she was sitting on between her fingers. Her cell phone rang part way through the dream, and her dream self looked down at the screen.

Jack.

Mia shook her head and hit *ignore.*

Then her mother screamed.

Six men carried a piano across the driveway of her parents' house. They were men built like barbarians—their arms as wide as kegs and legs as tall as trees. As they approached Mia, one of the men tripped on a turtle statue in the grass and he fell.

The piano came crashing down, almost landing on the gigantic man, and out rolled a body—a body that jiggled like gelatin. Mia screamed as the body rolled closer, stopping only inches from her face. There, Jack stared at her, his eyes dead.

Someone grabbed her from behind, pulling her away from the body, but the rancid smell entered her lungs, nonetheless.

Jack opened his mouth, a brown cloud leaving his lips before saying, "*Save me.*"

Mia woke to the dark room, her heart heavy in her ears. She tried to calm her breathing, and realized the feeling of being held did not leave with her dream.

"*I've killed at least fifty people.*"

Carl held Mia from behind, keeping her body close to his. Mia stiffened. The feeling of his breath on the side of her face was enough to make her scream, but his hand had slipped over her body and laid over her mouth. She could feel the rough scarring on her lips.

He took a deep breath and continued: "*Men. Women. Even a few kids. All across America. These highways have harbored my crimes for over three decades.*"

Mia nodded, trembling.

"*And I've* never *been caught.*"

They lay in silence for a few minutes. Mia breathed quick, shallow breaths through her nose, fearful she was going to pass out.

"*I could never kill you though.*"

Mia tried to get a look at Carl's face without moving her head, her eyes straining to see, but he was too far behind her.

His grip on her mouth tightened, and the hand on her hip clenched.

"*You're a good girl on a mission, and we have to get you back to California. With all you've been through, you don't deserve to die.*"

Mia's mind tried to wrap around his words, but all she could do was cry. Carl removed his hand from her mouth and hugged her tightly before letting go and retreating off the bed. Mia covered her face and sobbed quietly, fearful of being too loud.

Carl was snoring shortly after. Mia lay frozen in bed like a child fearful of monsters in the dark. She pretended the covers would be enough to protect her, covering her head with her blanket, and fell asleep.

Chapter Ten: Food for Worms

A maggot writhed its way down from his eye into his mouth at a steady pace. From his lip, it inched onto the inside of his cheek and scraped away at the tender flesh, alongside hundreds of others of its kind. Deryk's severed head sat on the porch in the shine of the winter sun. The coagulated blood puddle surrounding it pulsed with maggots. The air around it buzzed with flies. Nothing but piles of larvae filled his eye sockets.

The rest of his body lay in chunks around the patio furniture, each with its own hoard of hungry insects. A hand on the table. A foot on a chair. His penis drying on the patio's railing.

Rochelle pushed the sliding glass door open, the smell of rotten death permeating her senses. She smiled, the same smile she'd been smiling for days, and looked around at each piece. Like a woman in a grocery store, she inspected each hunk of meat carefully. A chunk of thigh meat caught her attention. How the maggots had formed a layer on the exposed muscle made for an astounding, eye-catching piece.

This will be the one.

She delicately picked it up and carried it inside, and bypassing the kitchen, she made a dash for Jack's recording room. There, Jack sat in his chair, trembling. He hadn't stopped shaking for the past few days. Between Rochelle's mania and her refusal to feed him, he felt perpetually on edge.

Excitement built in Rochelle's core. She set the meat down on a clean plate in front of Jack, much to his horror. Quickly moving out of the way, she adjusted the phone to capture the moment and clicked on the ring lights that used to bring Jack joy and what he believed was a genuine connection with his online following.

Jack looked down at the bundle of maggots before him, and picking up his fork, he leaned in to poke them.

"*Don't touch it*," Rochelle snapped.

Jack glanced up, catching her eyes. He held eye contact despite his tremors.

"Today's video is a mystery meat." Her smile returned to her lips. "You will eat this slowly. You *will* swallow some of the maggots whole. And—"

"*Whole?*" Jack interrupted, dropping his fork onto the plate with a clank.

"*Yes.*"

The way her voice deepened tightened Jack's lips, sealing them from further intervention.

"Your viewers will love it and engagement will skyrocket as you ask them to guess what sort of meat it is." She stood back, viewing Jack through the screen of his phone. "*It's perfect.*"

She opened Jack's channel and hit the *live stream* button.

"*And action.*"

Viewers clambered into Jack's live stream, curious about his lack of activity and sudden change in lifestyle. When greeted with his usual setup—tainted by dread and what appeared to be moving food—viewers were compelled to comment their joy, curiosity, and outright disgust.

Jack felt disheartened not being able to see the number of views or likes. He wanted to ask Rochelle to turn the phone around but feared her too much to do so. In an attempt to relight the flame he used to have for mukbang, he began his routine.

When his eyes flicked to the camera, many viewers jumped. Deep, dark circles had formed around Jack's eyes and his skin had lost much of its liveliness, sagging more than usual. He appeared to be a demented form of himself, or at least what viewers knew him as.

"*Hi, guys! Today we're going to be trying some mystery meat, ooo.*" He paused as if waiting for applause. "*In some countries—I don't know where—but uh—it's a delicacy to eat live maggots. So, let's get into it!*"

The excitement of his intro quickly wore off as he picked up his knife and fork and eyeballed his steak. It'd been days since the incident, and he was sure it was Deryk sitting before him.

Deryk and about a hundred maggots.

The sour taste of bile coated his dry tongue, and he struggled to keep down whatever remained in his empty gut. He watched the maggots dance on the hunk of meat for almost an entire minute before Rochelle gently cleared her throat. Jack looked up to her. She laid a hand out flat and pointed her other hand's index finger into it, mouthing *now*.

Jack adjusted the knife, noticing how it shook in his hand, and prepared to cut the meat as Rochelle watched the viewers pour in. Nudging some of the maggots out of the way with his knife, Jack could finally see how raw the meat was. He sawed into it, the texture being sinewy and gritty. Even the world's toughest steak would have been easier to cut. Crumbles of coagulated blood fell onto the plate along with squirming maggots with each pass of the blade.

When the knife clanked onto the ceramic, Jack jumped, a chunk of Deryk on his fork. He trembled and started to cry.

"*Hey,*" Rochelle snapped, under her breath.

Jack looked up to her.

"*Eat. It.*"

Jack took a deep breath, slowly pulling the meat to his lips. As he got closer to it, he could hear the maggots writhing. The potent smell of sour dirt and rot crawled through his nostrils and into the back of his throat. He vehemently shook his head.

"*Eat it!*" Rochelle yelled.

Jack shook his head, wishing it were Mia telling him to eat sausages that looked like dicks.

Rochelle pulled a kitchen knife from behind her back. She pointed the glinting blade at him, and screamed, "*EAT IT!*"

Jack could imagine the viewers' confusion. He wondered if any would call the police to save him from this nightmare.

Mia wondered the same thing the night before—if her parents would finally see all the missed calls and call the police—but being out on the road with Carl in the light of day, she felt safer. It could have been the sunlight, or it could have been that she'd stolen a men's razor from the lobby and tucked it up her sleeve.

Carl seemed to be in a genial mood. He told Mia he was just happy to drive somewhere that wasn't for a job. He'd turned the radio on, some country station that barely got reception, and drove Mia mad. Carl bounced the leg not on the accelerator as the music buzzed in between static. He was smirking when Mia got the idea to ask something wild.

"How does it feel to kill?" Her tone expressed nothing more than asking about the weather, but Carl's face fell slack at the words.

He side-eyed Mia, his knuckles turning white on the steering wheel.

"I once held a gun to my husband's head. It was only a few days ago in fact," She said. Again, her tone left nothing sinister in the air. It was all small talk.

The corners of Carl's lips turned down, and he nodded as he considered it. "Sounds about right."

"I thought about blowing his brains out against the walls."

"Uh-huh."

"But I couldn't."

"Why's that?"

Mia shrugged. "I guess—" she looked out her window at the brown fields around them, wondering when it had turned from snow to mud, "I guess I lost all strength in my trigger finger."

Carl guffawed, and Mia glared at him. "Don't take it personal, darlin'. You don't know how many people I've heard say that." He shook his head. "You started trembling and lost all strength in your core, and that's when you set the gun down."

Mia thought about it and nodded.

"You're not a coward. You're smart. You probably ran through all the possible outcomes in your mind without even realizing it and came to the subconscious decision that it wasn't worth it. Then your brain's conscious side became aware and told you to put the gun down." Carl shook his head. "I wish my brain would have done that the first time I robbed a liquor store."

"You robbed a liquor store?"

"Sure did. I was fifteen, with little more than a penny in my pocket. I robbed the place of seven hundred dollars straight from the cash register. I expected fifty, maybe seventy-five dollars from that register. When the cashier handed over a wad that fat, I didn't know how to react. He seemed to look me in the eye, past my mother's stocking that I wore, and I knew I had to kill him."

"Why?"

"He went to the same church my family did."

"Oh."

"So, I snatched the money, aimed the gun, and shot him in the forehead real quick. Any normal kid would have seen a familiar face, dropped the money, and ran. But not little Carl. No, Carl had new shoes and gifted his mother a nice necklace the next week with no questions asked because there was no one to ID me." He chuckled. "It's a good thing I was a teen before security cameras were in every store."

Mia sat in silence, watching cars drive by on the other side of the freeway as she thought about Carl's words. She wanted to hear more.

"I used to rob stores for the hell of it even once I got a job. I had plenty of money to spend on myself and my little sister but..." he trailed off, passing a semi-truck. Ahead of them, the clouds broke up into a bright blue sky. Mia looked in the passenger mirror, spotting the darkened storm clouds behind them. She hoped it was a metaphor of sorts.

Carl sighed. "But I didn't have any excitement. I lived for nothing. Saved for nothing. I felt there was no future for me, and committing crimes was the only thing that brought me any feeling."

He looked over at Mia, and she nodded, hoping he would continue.

"When my mother died, my sister moved to Alabama. We grew up in Illinois, so that was a far drive. I had the house all to myself. I had no friends, no girlfriend, no supervision, and a lot of pent-up feelings. I was mad at my mom for dying when I was only twenty. I was mad at my sister for leaving me. She was still a kid, but without Mom around, she wouldn't listen to me." Carl's voice seemed to strain, as if the feelings were as fresh as the day after his mother passed. "I was mad that I never had a dad, too. Mad that the son-of-a-bitch impregnated my mother as a teenager and bailed." He shook his head, not even seeming to pay attention to the road. "*I was mad that I was twenty and all alone.*"

Carl's foot slowly pressed harder on the accelerator as he spoke, and with his last sentence, he eased off of it, slowing to the speed limit. He sighed. "So, I went on a mission to find my father."

Mia thought about her own father and how she hadn't heard from her parents in days.

How many times have I called? she wondered.

Surely, they would call her. They'd call her and reassure her that everything was okay—and she'd get home to Jack safe and sound with Deryk there taking care of him. Jack just didn't answer and didn't call back because he was taking a break from his phone.

Surely. Surely that's right.

"—and I knocked on that motherfucker's door hard as the police!" Carl said.

Mia came to from her own thoughts as the pain in her thighs finally reached her threshold. She unclenched her hands, removing her fingernails from the flesh under her sweatpants.

"He'd been in the living room smoking and watching TV. I could see the flicker through the window. When he opened the door, it was like *bam*."

"Yeah?"

"Yeah, it was like meeting my twin for the first time. I couldn't be mad at a face like his."

"Mmmhmm."

"But he had already seen the gun in my hand, and there was no turning back."

No turning back.

Mia shook her head, her eyes full of that bright blue sky ahead of them. She had a feeling in her heart, a strong one that said,

Your life will never be the same.

The maggots crunched under Jack's teeth, bursting bitter juices between the grinding bones. He had taken his front teeth and scraped a few off the meat to get a taste of just the maggots. They had squirmed on his tongue for a half a second before he shoved them under his teeth, sending a chill down his spine.

Jack's head hurt—whether it was from the lights, starvation, or the pure terror he felt, he did not know. His entire body shook and glistened under the powerful lights. An internal conflict filled him.

Rochelle stared on, her thighs tingling. She thought about the man down in Southern California, and how his body might look now. How she could scrape his coagulated blood from the floor and shovel it into Jack's mouth.

He would chew it and swallow it like the pig that he is, she thought.

She had set down the knife as soon as Jack took a bite, placing it on another table in the room. The followers and viewers and comments and likes were all forgotten in this moment of triumph. Rochelle grinned as Jack opened his mouth further, encapsulating an *entire* chunk of Deryk. Her head rushed as his lips closed over the fork and he pulled it away.

In one swallow, it was down his gullet.

Rochelle huffed and shook her head. She pointed to her face and chewed the air furiously. Jack pretended he didn't see, opting to cut himself another bite. It wasn't nearly as bad as he'd expected. Half his taste was gone, so, although the meat was sour, the maggots gave it an almost sweet, creamy taste.

Jack wondered if he'd feel the same about this meat had he not been starved.

Rochelle bared her teeth and whispered, "*Chew it.*"

Jack took a deep breath and made what he thought was eye contact with one of the maggots on the plate. He could imagine the maggots chowing down on the chunk, having their own feast, as he prepared to cut into it. Jack would feast upon the feast, the nasty bits and all.

He sawed through and picked it up. His stomach growled— loudly. He looked at the camera, thinking of all the people watching and laughing at him, and took a bite. Jack chewed the stringy meat, revulsed by the chill on his tongue. Maggots popped under his teeth, and he thought he could hear their screams. How he wished he could scream with them.

Mia screamed with laughter as Carl hollered from the driver's seat. He had continued onto even darker stories from his childhood.

"*I told her! I told her my dog was messed up!*" He bounced up and down as he yelled.

Mia laughed harder, gripping her stomach and imagining the girl's face as she saw Carl's mutilated dog.

"*I done told her that the neighbor came over and gave him a permanent smile. She just stood there, looking at his scabby, wide grin. Then she gagged! Damn near threw up the lunch I just bought her all over my mother's rug!*"

Mia cackled from the passenger seat, throwing her head back and pinching her stomach. Not even the sharp pain of her nails could get her to stop.

She could see the dog, mangled and mutilated by disgruntled neighbors. The long white fur had been stained red, as were Carl's words, and it made Mia sick. She clenched her esophagus as she laughed, trying to keep down whatever stomach bile was left in her gut. Tears streamed down her face.

Carl drove through the California border, speeding right past the man standing at the booth who waved cars on with a smile. He had plenty of stories to tell in the little time they had left together.

Mia laughed on, wishing she could stop. She thought about opening the creaky truck door and launching herself out onto the asphalt. She wondered just how hard it would hurt and how far she would roll before her skin pulled away from muscle and her muscle pulled away from bone. She wondered how far her blood would travel, and she wondered what would be left of her. She wondered if it would stop all the madness inside her brain, and she laughed on.

Rochelle's cheeks hurt from the smile on her lips. Jack was on his last bite.

His stomach writhed, from nausea or living maggots, he did not know. His skin prickled as Rochelle had cranked up the heater. His rolls dripped sweat and a few squirming maggots.

Eat it and it'll be over. She'll shut off the camera and it'll all be over.

Jack's hand trembled as he pulled the fork closer. His body hurt from shaking the entire duration of the video. He opened his mouth and welcomed the *mystery meat*. Maggots danced on his tongue before he pushed them under his teeth and ground into them.

On this last bite, one maggot squelched, leaking bitter juices on his tongue. The others had been sweet and creamy, so he wondered what was wrong with this one. Jack cringed, chewing the meat and swallowing.

He took a second to breathe evenly, trying to stop his gut from pushing everything up his esophagus. He would spray the table with bile, rotted meat, and maggot mush if he wasn't careful, and he wasn't sure what Rochelle would do. His eyes averted from the camera, opting to stare out the window at the pines outside. It had been weeks since he had been outside.

Rochelle snapped her fingers, bringing his attention to her. She pointed at her mouth and pretended to speak. He couldn't figure out what she was saying, but figured she wanted him to do his ending.

Jack faced the camera, faked a smile, and said, "*Mmm, that was some good mystery meat. Be sure to comment what you think it is! Bye-bye!*"

Jack hated himself. He hated the man he'd become and realized with those baby words exactly the man he'd become. His eyes bore into Rochelle. His *number one fan*. She was to blame for the way he'd become. She and thousands upon thousands of other fucks who encouraged this shit, who got off to it.

As much as Jack feared Rochelle, he'd grown to hate her just as much.

Mia saw the sign she had passed many times before, the third exit before hers. She perked up in her seat, anxious to be back in the place she once considered her prison.

Do prisoners miss the wardens?

She wondered about it and doubted it just as quickly.

Rochelle smiled and tapped the screen, shutting off the live stream. Without a word, she picked up the plate, flung the remaining maggots on Jack, and left the room.

Jack gasped as they rained on him. He smacked them away, swiping at his gelatinous body. They rolled and squirmed on his damp skin, sticking and clinging to the sweat. He could feel them on his bald head, between his rolls, and in his pants. Taking a deep breath, one rolled down his forehead and got sucked into his maw. Jack coughed, hoping to get the larva out of his windpipe. It flung forward in his throat and found its way into his esophagus, where Jack swallowed it whole.

Focused on getting the maggots out of his shorts, he didn't notice the one crawling down the side of his head.

He pulled up his gut as far as he could, noticing the maggots already under the skin.

Were they there before?

The skin was red and inflamed, and what he'd mistaken for irritation from Deryk's cleaning, was maggots feasting on his tender flesh. He stared at the hoard in awe, watching as they swam around in his pus-filled under-cavity. With his free hand, he opened his shorts.

He gasped.

The raw flesh of his penis was coated in writhing maggots. Blood stained his white underwear, and Jack could see maggot-filled craters which seeped blood. Distracted by his half-dead penis, Jack didn't feel the maggot crawl into his ear.

It inched its way through his ear canal, scraping away ear wax as it went.

Jack looked up, feeling something move in his ear. Hearing what sounded like paper crinkling in his head, his eyes widened. He poked at his ear with his index finger, plugging it. When the movement didn't cease, Jack realized what was inside his head.

Taking another deep breath, he screamed.

Rochelle sat outside in the dirt, barefoot. She held a small shovel in her hand, something she found in the dead garden on the side of the house. Digging in the damp dirt, she plucked free worms and trapped them in a mason jar she'd also found on the side of the house. The jar was already half full, and she had a special dish in mind for Jack.

She thought back to her childhood. Full of abuse from her father, she'd always found comfort in doing the things she knew she wasn't supposed to do.

She liked digging up worms and eating them or putting them in other people's food.

As a ten-year-old, she'd run away to the forest with her dad's big Bowie knife, and kill anything in her path. She'd pretend the small animals were all the people who hurt her in life. Killing squirrels and rodents, she'd roast them on a fire, eating them half raw. Her favorite part was plucking free the tiny organs and eating them whole. She'd carve open the animals and smear herself in their blood. Her mom would find her, covered in mud and blood, in the backyard days later.

She shook her head as she carefully plucked another worm free. There was a jar of old spaghetti sauce in the pantry she'd seen earlier.

Would he even notice the difference?

Rochelle stood up, her knees muddy. She wore Mia's pajamas, which were about four sizes too small. The string on the pants had receded into them completely, and they pinched her waist. The shirt fit snugly against her large breasts and plump stomach, leaving three inches of her abdomen exposed.

She carried the jar inside to the sink. Upstairs, Jack sobbed loudly. Rochelle carefully filled the jar with water and dumped out the mud between her fingers until the water she dumped out ran clean. She pinched a worm between her fingers and pulled it out of the jar. Lifting it to her mouth, she smiled and sucked in the worm like a spaghetti noodle. Her teeth ground through the chewy, gritty worm, and as she swallowed, she could feel one of the segments writhing.

"*Rochelle!*" Jack cried.

She set down the jar and rushed upstairs. A gasp escaped her when she entered the room.

Blood dribbled down Jack's cheek and from his rolls. His skin appeared to move, but as she drew closer, she realized that the maggots she'd thrown on him earlier were multiplying.

Flies buzzed around the room in a haze of rotten filth.

"What's the matter, Jack?" Something deep inside her told Rochelle this was wrong, but the lusting voice in her head pushed it down.

Jack's eyes were bloodshot from crying, and his skin was yellow and red. Some of the red patches seemed to puddle in his skin like deep bruises, almost glowing. He looked up to Rochelle from his chair and let out a shaky sigh.

"Just kill me already."

"What?" Rochelle asked. She oddly found Jack more attractive this way. If she could get a human brain put on his plate, why—

He'd be like a zombie. Like a hot, dead zombie.

"I thought you cared about me?" Jack said, hot tears streaming down his sticky skin. "I thought you cared?"

"Well, I do care about sex, and I do like guys."

Jack shook his head, a maggot falling off his face and rolling down his chest.

"And you're a guy," she paused, smirking, and continued, "a guy with a penis that, well, it's got to be girthy right?"

He shook his head harder, his face contorting into a grimace. He glared at Rochelle. "*You want to see it? You want to see my* girthy *cock?*" he yelled, his voice cracking on *cock*.

Rochelle smiled and came closer. The sour stench grew worse as she approached him. She bowed her head down as Jack lifted his stomach.

"Go ahead, pull my pants down."

Rochelle gently put her fingers on the hem of his shorts, taking her time. She pulled down slowly when Jack called out.

"*Hurry up!*" His arms shook as he struggled to keep his stomach up.

Rochelle yanked his pants down and was struck with the sight of his maggot infested penis. The thought of wrapping her lips around it and feeling the larvae swim around on her tongue ran through her mind. Conflicting feelings followed before she snapped the shorts back and pulled her hand away.

Jack let his stomach down, like the hood of a car, and nodded. "Disgusting, right? I'm just a pile of bugs and blubber now!" He slammed his fist onto the table. "*Fuck!*" Grabbing Rochelle by the arm, he yanked her closer.

Her nose almost touched his, and through her fear and arousal, she thought she could see something moving in the white of Jack's eye. Something small and squirmy.

"*You still wanna fuck me?*"

Rochelle pulled away. "I—I mean—"

"*Ew!*" Jack shoved the table over, the legs sprawling into the air. "*That's all you wanted me for!*"

Rochelle leaned toward him, jabbing her finger in his face. "*That's all you wanted me for, too!*"

"*You want to infest your pussy with maggots?!*"

Rochelle backed away, the smell making her stomach do cartwheels. She thought about douching her vagina to get rid of the maggots, watching them flush out onto her thighs, and shook her head.

She took another step away from Jack and slipped. Distracted by Jack's *girth*, she didn't notice she had stepped barefoot through his feces which soaked the carpet. Her head hit the floor with a thud.

"Yeah, I've been shitting and pissing myself in here because you won't help me!"

"I—" Rochelle looked around, the arousal gone. Her mind was stone cold and the shit burned her nostrils. She looked up to Jack, still lying in the swamp of his feces. "You're not what I want anymore."

She stood up and left the room, heading into the guest bathroom downstairs. Once inside, she peeled off Mia's pajamas and jumped into the shower. Thoughts raced through her mind louder than the water.

Someone will look for him,
and when they do,
he'll tell them it was you.

"Do you regret killing your dad, Carl?" she asked tentatively, as if her words were stepping around landmines.

"Mmm," Carl started, "I don't." He nodded, affirming this.

"Mmm," Mia said, also nodding.

After this long and weird journey with him, she began to think of Carl as a protective father figure, despite his confessions. Her own father—and even her mother—were known to fold to other people's wants and needs. She didn't blame them for shutting down the restaurant, but at the same time, she felt they could have done more to combat the people attacking them.

Just like you could have done more to prevent all of this. Like parent, like daughter.

Mia shook her head. It ached in a way she couldn't explain.

"Do you regret leaving Jack?" Carl asked softly, almost as if he was scared to ask.

The second closest exit sign to hers passed by. Only two more to go. She felt goosebumps break out on her skin.

"I do."

"I do!" Mia yelled.

Jack said, "I do," under his breath with his and her parents watching from the small pews of the church Mia had grown accustomed to. Jack and his family flew out to North Carolina to allow Mia to have her dream wedding despite living across the country.

The night passed in agony as Jack's mother clung to him and interrupted Mia's speech.

Sandra, Jack's mother, spoke of how much she would miss her boy during her toast. Mia had assured her they would visit often, only to be met with a sharp glare.

Jack fell asleep early during their first night as a married couple, and Mia ran the night through her mind over and over in the darkness, wondering what she had done.

Sitting in the passenger seat of Carl's truck, Mia replayed this moment in her mind, wishing Jack's mother would have objected to the wedding like Mia knew she wanted to.

You could have left at any time.

She nodded, agreeing with the voice in her head. It was spiteful, but it was right.

I left him, only filling myself with regret. What do you think of that? she asked the voice.

Silence.

She imagined Jack having fallen down the stairs again, or the nurse improperly securing his CPAP machine. She even imagined him choking to death on one of the sausages still in the fridge.

What have I done?

"You did what you had to do, darlin'," Carl said under his breath.

Tears streamed down her cheeks as the next exit sign flew by.

One more to go.

"*I'm going to have to execute him*," Rochelle said to the mirror. Beads of sweat littered her brow. Her body was damp, but her fingers were drenched. Vomit had splattered up her legs after her lengthy shower, a result of her finger fucking session.

She'd thrusted them deeper and deeper, feeling a sense of pleasure as well as revulsion. As she stuck her fingers in and pulsed them front to back, she could envision Jack's maggot infested penis penetrating her. The maggots would writhe inside her, crawling toward her uterus like a hoard of sperm, eager for the warm, wet safe haven.

She could see herself straddling his large thighs, bouncing up and down, but when within her vision, she saw his face, all attraction was lost.

Her fingers grew weak as she lost all drive to orgasm. The maggots and bloody, pus-covered penis would do all by itself, but Jack's ugly mug wouldn't do.

In the kitchen sat a knife—a knife still covered in Deryk's blood. It was plenty sharp.

Rochelle left the bathroom, entirely naked and still spattered in vomit, and whipped down the hallway.

"*Please just speed up, Carl!*"

"*I'm going eighty-five as it is!*" he yelled, his voice hoarse.

Mia trembled in the passenger seat, her hands gripping the dash. Jack was dead. She knew it. Deep in her heart, she knew he was dead, and she wanted to see his body before he decayed completely.

It's all your fault. You had to try to see Mommy and Daddy.

"*Shut up!*" she screamed, letting go of the dash and pulling at her short hair.

Rochelle bounded up the stairs, her breasts and stomach jiggling up and down in unison, her wet hair slapping against her bare back. The knife twinkled in her hand as she thrust it forward with each step.

"*Kee-yah!*" she whispered, jabbing it forward. "*Take that!*" she said, envisioning her father. He'd grown heavy-set and pale toward the end of his life, and having lost all his hair to cancer, one would say he resembled Jack in his current state—all except that maggoty unit of his.

"*Rochelle!*" Jack called.

He could feel each maggot under his skin. Every scrape of their miniscule mouths tore a fresh lightning bolt of pain through his nervous system. They pulsed around his penis, like an intricate set of roots cinching down on it.

They're going to chew it off, he thought as Rochelle pounced into the room.

"*JaAack!*" she screeched, wielding the knife in both fists.

Jack screamed.

"*Turn here! Turn here!*" Mia shrieked.

Carl whipped the truck onto a narrow asphalt road, having left the freeway only moments ago.

"*Go as fast as you can!*"

Carl shook his head, pressing the pedal to the floor. The truck roared, pine trees flying by on either side of them.

"*Rochelle! I'm telling you—you* don't *have to do this!*"

Jack batted at her with weak, heavy arms as she tore at his shorts. She shoved aside his stomach flap violently.

Barefoot in a sea of crusty feces, Rochelle gripped Jack. Maggots writhed under her fingers.

She lined up the knife at the base of his cock.

"*This one! This one!*"

Carl's tires squealed on the asphalt as he came to an abrupt stop. He turned into the driveway, certain the truck was going to flip.

"*Here! Hurry!*"

What if you're overreacting? What if he's fine?

Deryk's car isn't here.

Her eyes widened.

Something's wrong.

"*Rochelle!*" Jack shoved at her head as she took the first cut into his skin.

The knife slipped, narrowly missing Rochelle's fingers. Rochelle pulled her head back, and with a grunt, she slammed her forehead into Jack's nose.

A spray of blood showered her face, and she readjusted her grip on his dick. With the precision of a chef, she slid the knife halfway through the shaft.

Jack cried out.

Mia opened the door before Carl slowed to a stop. She threw herself out, almost smashing herself into the door before bolting for the house.

"*Jack!*" she screamed.

His screams echoed out into the forest surrounding their home.

Rochelle held with an iron grip as she tore the knife through the rubbery flesh. Hot excitement burned through her, fueling her final move. Pulling upward, she sawed the blade through in one swift move.

She held her prize high in the air like a goblet dripping wine.

Jack looked up in awe, his lips tightly shut.

The front door was unlocked, allowing Mia into the horror scene that was her kitchen. She stumbled in, the only sound in her ears being Jack's cries. Dried blood coated the floor. She stifled a scream as Jack went silent.

"*Jack!*" she yelled, her voice cracking. Tears streamed down her face as she ran to the stairs. The hand gripping the banister trembled.

Carl got out of the truck, leaving it idling in the cold. The screams penetrated his mind, sending a flood of memories to the forefront of his attention.

Rochelle jumped at the sound of Mia's voice. She held the severed penis close against her chest and ducked into Jack's bedroom.

It took Jack a few moments to register Mia's voice through his haze of shock. When she screamed again, he first mistook her for an angel—one he was sure was going to take off with him at any moment.

By the third shout, he knew who it was.

"*Mia!*" His arms aimlessly reached out as his vision narrowed. Darkness encroached upon it.

"*Jack!*" Mia clambered up the stairs as Rochelle ducked into the walk-in closet, knife and penis in hand.

She silently closed the door and dropped the knife. Her legs shook as she held the flaccid penis in both hands.

Mia flew through the door of the recording room, stunned. A puddle of shit and piss slowly expanded into the fibers of the carpet with Jack's flowing blood. She carefully made her way around the upturned table.

Jack's eyes finally focused on her, and he gasped.

"*Get my...penis...Rochelle.*"

Mia glanced at Jack's crotch, and her blood ran cold.

Apparently, he doesn't bleed ice cream.

Mia shook her head. "*Rochelle?!*"

Oh my god that obsessive bitch is in the house.

Rochelle breathed heavily, holding it by its base. She got down on her hands and knees, spreading her thighs.

"*Bedroom,*" Jack whispered.

Mia was torn between getting his dick back and trying to stem the bleeding. She smacked at her pockets, realizing her phone was in Carl's truck.

"Put pressure on your crotch, Jack," she said. His eyes wandered about, making it hard for her to make eye contact. "Do it, okay?"

Jack focused on her words and slowly moved his arms to his stomach. He wiggled his fingers underneath and pushed with as much force as he could.

Mia nodded and ran from the recording room into the bedroom.

Empty.

Mia slowly stepped through the room, passing by the walk-in closet.

A trembling sigh caught her attention.

Mia whipped open the door and screamed.

Quivering, Rochelle held the penis between her thighs, only an inch from penetrating herself. Tears streamed from her eyes as she looked up at Mia. Opening her mouth, a whisper escaped.

"*I can't do it.*" She softly shook her head, her gaze falling to the carpet, defeated.

"*What—what the fuck?!*" Mia shoved Rochelle to the side and snatched it from her hands.

Rochelle fell to the side, gave up the penis, and crawled out of the closet.

Movement tickled Mia's fingers, and upon looking at the severed meat, she realized it was *alive.*

Alive with maggots of an unnatural red and yellow.

She dropped it and quickly picked it back up as Rochelle darted out of the bedroom.

"*Get back here, you bitch!*" Mia roared, chasing after her.

Rochelle bounded down the stairs, her naked body slick with blood. The open door was her light at the end of the tunnel.

Where will I go from here? she wondered.

Anywhere, she assured herself.

Mia thudded down the stairs after her, careful not to drop Jack's penis again.

"Carl! Call the police!"

Carl had been leaning against the grill of his truck when Mia's voice startled him. A naked, bloody woman ran out of the front door and down the driveway.

Carl's vision centered wholly on her. His heart slowed as he took long strides toward her.

Rochelle's heart beat heavy in her ears as she ran. She noticed the lean old man approaching her and was determined to plow through him.

Within feet of each other, Carl stepped aside and reached his left arm out, hooking Rochelle's neck. She grunted as he forced his arm in a lock around her neck. His right hand popped a button on the sheath on his hip, and out came his revered Bowie. It glinted in the sunlight as Mia made her way outside.

In a movement as swift as Rochelle's, Carl slid the Bowie across her neck, dropping her. Blood fountained from Rochelle's throat, and she collapsed to the gravel, convulsing. Sucking sounds came from her body as she clawed at the wound.

Mia looked at Carl, stunned, before diving back into the house.

"Jack!" she screamed, rushing up the stairs again. *"Jack!"*
Silence.

Her arms reached out for the doorway, and on the approach, she grabbed the doorframe to the recording room, launching herself inside.

Jack's head sat at an angle, and he stared at her with bloodshot eyes.

"Oh my God."

She carefully walked through the puddles of excrement and tentatively placed a hand on his neck.

He's already cold.

His lap dripped blood as the carpet coagulated.

Tears sprouted in her eyes, and she covered her face in her hands. A cry escaped her throat, and she turned, running out of the room.

Carl bent down, wiping his blade on Rochelle's side, when Mia popped out of the front door.

"*Carl, he's dead*," she said.

He'd never seen her appear so small. His heart ached for her in a way he'd never felt before. Having nothing else to say, he said, "Let's get out of here, darlin'."

Afterword – September 2023

This book was supposed to be published Christmas 2022. I wrote 50k words of it for National Novel Writing Month (November), then I was struck with writer's block. The ending took me three months to finally write. I wrote it one afternoon in the sun, pen on paper. Writing on paper instead of typing on the computer sometimes helps me with writer's block.

Well, a good gust of wind took seven pieces of paper (fourteen pages of writing) right off the table while I was out teaching my neighbor's son to skateboard. My dog, Kraig, loves paper and cardboard.

The ending was never found.

The only thing that remained was the clip I used to hold the pieces of paper together.

I was so upset. I was ready to quit writing. I was ready to quit life.

Twenty-four hours later, I laughed because that ending *sucked*. It was sappy and rushed. The first draft after a bout of writer's block surely shouldn't be the *ending* of my novel, right? So, I put my big girl panties on and got to writing again. I made it more gruesome and disgusting, and gave Mia a harsher reality to live with, one where she doesn't get to console Jack as he dies. It's what she needed...

Well, as I began to write this, I realized I lost the series title. Yes, this is a *series*, and months ago I had come up with a very clever name. Whether or not what I decided to name this series yesterday is the same name that I came up with prior, the world may never know. I need to stop using a whiteboard for such important notes…

I think the largest power against this book was my own self doubt. I have a chronic illness which causes depression and anxiety. Lots of that seep into my own creative projects, and I'm left with an unsatiated feeling after the completion of a project. Hindsight is 20/20, and I dwell on all the things I've done wrong. I know so because I've done so for the last five books I published.

What will people think of the story?
What if the message comes across wrong?
What if they don't understand where I'm coming from?'
Will people think I'm a bad person?
What if readers ridicule me and my skill?

And the questions go on, swimming and spinning around in my head, while I shower, while I eat, while I watch TV, and even in my dreams. It, and I, never feels good enough. If it weren't for my impulsiveness, my projects would sit in a folder on my computer and be edited into oblivion.

Despite all of this and more:

I completed the book. I promoted it. I self-published it. I even illustrated the fucking thing.

By the time you read this, hopefully I'll have sold a million copies and have international fame. If that's not the case, trust me, I'm working on it.

I appreciate you much more than you know, whether I know you personally or not. You've chosen to spend a few hours in my head, shit, you spent money to be in my head, and I can't thank you enough for sharing your time with me. Writing is how I express myself, and I don't think readers understand just how much of myself I put into all of my characters, or maybe you do. Either way, I thank you from my bottom, or whatever the phrase is–bottom of my heart? Yeah, I thank you from the bottom of my heart for taking the time to get to know me a little better.

Acknowledgements

Thank you to my editor, Patrick C. Harrison III. I can't thank him enough for accepting this piece of hot garbage and giving me usable feedback and criticisms. I did not realize how often I say "that" and "had" until he pointed it out about a thousand times in the first revision. Embarrassing. I was entirely surprised and thrilled that one of my favorite indie authors wanted to edit my work. The phone call which ensued the edits was one of the highlights of my career. Patrick reassured my abilities as a writer in a very dim moment in my life, and, again, I can't thank him enough.

Thank you to my beta reader and good friend, Damien Lee. He helped me look over the manuscript one last time, and without him this book would be full of en dashes instead of em dashes! Apparently I read a lot of British literature as a kid because I spell a lot of things the English way, and I'm glad Damien was able to point this out to me! He was another reassuring voice that I desperately needed on this journey, and one of the first eyes to read this manuscript.

Thank you to one of my best friends, Fallon Raynes. An author herself, Fallon has always been very supportive of me, especially when I'm down on myself. She was yet another reassuring voice that I needed to keep me going.

I may not have space for all the names, but if we had a positive interaction from October 2022 through September

2023, then you made an impact on this book and whether it would be published, even if you didn't realize it. As a creator with depression and a chronic illness, my self-doubt leaches into my projects, and sometimes they're hanging on by a thread. I was very nervous to let this book into the world because I did cover topics I haven't yet. I was so scared. But everyone throughout the entire process was so supportive, save for those hateful few, and those few voices were trampled by the support of my fellow authors and friends. I can't say it enough: thank you ♥

PS

Need I even mention my parents, whom I dedicated my very first book to? I think it goes without saying that without them, there wouldn't be a me. There wouldn't be a dork on the internet making weird videos about cannibals, and there wouldn't be the book in your hands. Without them I am nothing, and to them I owe the world. This book is for them, as is every other piece of art I create. To them, I dedicate my entire career because they have been so unabashedly supportive.

Thank you, Mom and Dad.

Look Ma, I'm in the back of a book!
Usually these are in third person, but fuck that. Hi, I'm Author
Alyanna Poe, and you might have noticed that I write horror.
I've been writing horror since I was about thirteen, and I don't
plan on stopping anytime soon. I live in Northern California
and sometimes Nevada. I love small towns where I can feel
anonymous, so I don't plan on sticking around one place too
long. By the time you read this, I might just be on a colony on
Mars. Who knows?
My favorite hobbies include: drawing, petting my dogs,
blowing out my eardrums with music, and watching people's
reactions when I tell them I was born in 2001.

You can check out my other books here:
authoralyannapoe.com
And follow me on Instagram where I post creepy cannibal fun
facts:
@authoralyannapoe
Thanks again for believing in my work. I hope you enjoyed
MUKBANG, and even if you didn't, please leave an honest
review on places like Amazon, GoodReads, and your social
media. Every review helps, even the ones talking shit! XD

Photos circa 2025 by Alyanna Poe